Monarch
Moon

BONNIE K. TESH

Publishing Coordinator–Sharon Kizziah-Holmes
Cover Design – Jaycee DeLorenzo

Paperback-Press
an imprint of A & S Publishing
Paperback Press, LLC
Springfield, Missouri

ISBN - 978-1-964559-16-2

Dedication

This book would not be possible without the love and support of my husband and best friend, Richard (Dick) Tesh. It takes a strong person to put up with a writer, especially this one. The 1984 Mustang convertible in this novel is real. Dick came home one day and asked if I would mind if he bought a convertible. He found it behind someone's house, misused and abused. It needed some TLC. The man completely rebuilt the car. She looked brand new when he finished. We no longer own her, but we spent many hours driving the Ozark Mountain roads around Table Rock Lake, Missouri, in that sweet little blue gem.

So, thank you, sweetheart, for being patient with this crazy wife, keeping me fed and watered while I wrote this novel, and thank you for giving me this wonderful character for my book. I love you.

Acknowledgements

If I mentioned every person instrumental in getting Monarch Moon from my brain to the finished product, it would take an additional book. The names here are the tip of the iceberg.

Thanks go to Duke Pennell for the final edit. He went the extra mile by sharing his expertise in law enforcement and other fields. I appreciate his thoroughness.

Sharon Kizziah-Holmes at Paperback Press guided me through the publication process with a gentle hand and turned a manuscript into this book.

Jaycee DeLorenzo, of Sweet and Spicy Designs, came up with a beautiful cover. She is amazing!

Barbara Pearson and Jeanie Horn did preliminary editing. Sadly, we lost Jeanie a few years ago. I miss her.

Three critique groups gave me great feedback and constructive criticism. My Prose Sisters, Margarite Stever and April Brock, were with me from the beginning page to the last over the course of a year. They have a special place in my heart. John Caulfield, writing as J.C. Fields, has been an amazing critique partner, mentor, and friend.

Diane Yates shared her expertise with me throughout the process, and Ronda Del Boccio gave me great one-on-one feedback.

I must thank Summer and Claudia for their input, and my buddy and critique partner, John Daleske, for his support and kindness. I miss him.

Most of all, I thank my husband, Richard, for his constant support of my writing. Without him, I could not do what I do.

To our kids and grandkids, John, Candi, Missy, Michael, Shelbie, Taylor, and Dalton. Thank you for being the special people you are, for loving and supporting me.

Chapter 1

Some mistakes in this life, girl, you never quit paying for.

Her Texas mama's words beat at Rally like a drum.

Even with the top down, the wind could not drown out that voice in her head. She had shrugged off the warnings when she was younger, but now she understood. A past mistake propelled her out of Chicago in the middle of the night toward the Ozark Mountains of Missouri.

The fall evening was crisp and clear, a tonic to her worries. A thick wool sweater and a cozy knit scarf staved off the cool air, except for a slight chill nipping at her ankles. Before she left town, she had wavered on whether to raise the convertible top, but she liked to drive with a clear view of the star-studded sky.

Had she made the wrong choice in letting Joe Fenner live? Was that one of those mistakes she would never quit paying for? She stared at a ribbon of black highway and worried the small scar over her right carotid artery with her fingertips, a memento from the tip of her attacker's knife. She shivered, but not from the cold. The world was harsh, and she would need to get tough to survive. Next time, she would shoot to kill.

~ ~ ~ ~

Pale light cut into a dark horizon as she entered Hayes County, Missouri. She glanced at her Fossil watch. *Six twenty-three.*

When her best friend, Marney Phillips, moved to the Ozarks, she extended an open invitation for Rally to visit. She had debated about making the late-night call, but Marney seemed delighted.

After a stop at a convenience store for coffee and a snack, she found a park. Bright streaks of pinks and mauves covered the sky as the sun crept above the surrounding hills. The view was spectacular. She had heard the Ozarks were scenic, but she hadn't expected this. The brochure she grabbed at the convenience store described the terrain as mountainous. As she looked around, she understood why.

Her hands itched to get into the trunk and pull out a camera. She didn't want to call Marney yet, so she grabbed some equipment and wandered. It might help get Fenner's courtroom threat out of her mind.

Breathtaking views of an aquamarine river snaking through the valley below filled her camera lens and her mind. She finally checked the time, walked back to her car, loaded the equipment, then ripped open another bag of chips before getting behind the wheel.

The temptation to squeeze off a few extra shots as she pulled out of the overlook was too great to ignore. She grabbed her cell phone, held it at arm's length, and pointed it at an ethereal morning mist that hugged the side of a mountain.

Her powder blue 1984 Mustang convertible veered into the opposite lane of traffic and, before she could compensate, forced an oncoming vehicle to the shoulder. The car cut back onto the road and made a U-turn. The whine of a siren and the flash of rotating lights in her rearview mirror surprised her. She grimaced.

Great start, Rally. You called attention to yourself before you could even reach your destination.

She pulled onto the shoulder.

A tall man in a tan uniform and dark brown Stetson emerged from a patrol car and walked toward her. He stopped at the back of the Mustang, wrote on a clipboard, then walked to the front and stood by her door.

"Driver's license, proof of insurance, and registration, please."

She looked up. Dark, polarized sunglasses covered the officer's eyes. The Stetson's wide brim cut a shadow across his face and made it hard to read an expression. She opened the glove compartment, scattered contents around to cover a pink, holstered Beretta, then withdrew the documents.

"Oh, here it is." Her attempt at a smile received no response.

While the officer studied the information, she fumbled in her oyster Coach bag, retrieved a matching billfold, and sorted through several business cards, then put them back. A plastic sleeve on the side held pay dirt.

"Ah, right on top." She thrust the open wallet at the officer.

He handed the forms back to her, then motioned at the wallet. "Take the license out, please."

"Sure, okay." She slid the card from its pocket and handed it to him. While he looked at it, she brushed potato chip crumbs from her linen trousers, then pulled a napkin from the door well and wiped her hands.

He made notes on the clipboard. "This license is expired."

"What?" She shook her head and stared at his hand. "It can't be. I renewed it a few months ago."

"It's expired, ma'am. There's a hole punch here, and the date is—"

"Let me see that." She grabbed for the license, but the officer drew his hand back. He removed the sunglasses and stared at her.

Without his shades, she saw eyes as blue as the San Marcos River back home in Texas. "The license is …" She went swimming in them. "…valid."

He cleared his throat.

She focused her gaze back on the license and continued. "I passed the eye test, the whole drill. I had to take off work to go down to that miserable place. There were fifteen people ahead of me, but I stuck it out, made me late to my next photo shoot—"

"Ma'am." He stood stiff, like a statue.

"Yes?" She watched the corner of his mouth twitch. She took a deep breath, pushed an errant strand of hair away from her face. "I'm sorry, but you must be mistaken. Please, let me see it."

The officer turned the license toward her. She leaned forward, glanced at his nametag: *Woods, Deputy Sheriff*, then refocused. "Oh, I see the problem. That's an old picture. This one is expired."

He shifted his weight. A puff of air escaped his nostrils. Faint, but she heard it, like a bull considering a charge. Perhaps he was losing patience.

"Yes, ma'am. That's what I said." He straightened, pushed his shoulder blades back and did a slow neck roll.

"I have a new one."

"And where might it be?" He slid the sunglasses back onto his face and fixed them on her.

"Ah," she pointed at her purse. "In there…I think."

The officer sighed, dropped the clipboard to his side. "I'll wait."

She caught him doing a sweeping glance at the front and back seats while she riffled through her purse and again pulled cards out of her wallet and sorted through them.

"Here it is." She thrust the permit at him.

He took his time, made more notes on the clipboard. A car honked as it passed. The deputy glanced around, raised an arm in reply, studied the photo, then her.

So, my hair is a few shades lighter now. Hair always looks darker in photos. She pulled a strand from behind an ear and twisted it with her finger. *Sometime today, officer.*

"Down here on vacation?"

No, I got lost on my way to Mexico on a business trip. She faked a smile. "Not really a vacation. I'm visiting a friend. I'm supposed to be meeting her"—she tapped her watch — "in a few minutes."

"May I ask who you're visiting?" He handed the license back to her.

Rally stiffened. "Is that important?"

"I thought you might need directions." He smiled and tipped his hat. "I hope you enjoy your stay, Miss Chandler. I'm giving you a warning this time. No ticket." He nodded at the road behind him. "You almost caused an accident back there. I had to take the shoulder to avoid hitting you. You need to be careful. Pay complete attention to your driving."

He raised an eyebrow and focused on the cell phone in the passenger seat. "It might be safer for you and everyone else if you would stop and get out of the car to take your pictures."

"I did." *Thank you very much.* "At that roadside park back there, the one that overlooks the river."

She tossed the billfold back into her purse and started the car.

"Oh, that's not a river. That's Twisted Lake. It meanders around the base of the mountains. There's a dam between it and Paradise Lake, a larger body of water farther down." He nodded toward her phone in the passenger seat. "In case you're thinking about more pictures."

So, now he's a tour guide? Or is he stalling? Rally bit her lip.

"Try to be more careful, Miss Chandler." She caught a hint of a smile as he backed away from her car.

"Yeah, sure. Overwhelmed by the scenery, I guess." She liked the smile, even though he had an irritating manner. She would have to ask Marney about him.

"Have a pleasant visit, ma'am." He sauntered back toward his vehicle but stopped at the rear of the car. She leaned over the side to see what he was doing.

"Nice touch." He pointed at the small spray of bluebonnets painted on the driver's side fender with the words *Lupinus texensis* arched over it.

"Thanks. Some of my dad's artwork. He named her Blue Bonnet. I call her Blue."

Even with him walking away from her, there was no missing the soft chuckle that floated back in the clear morning air.

Chapter 2

C lay Woods got into his cruiser and watched as the little Mustang convertible pulled out onto the paved road and headed west. Rally Chandler might be more of a problem than he expected. She didn't know that Detective Scott Ketcham, who worked her case in Kansas City, had ties to the Ozarks. Clay's path crossed with his a few times at law enforcement meetings across the state.

When the detective heard that Joe Fenner escaped jail in a dirty laundry truck, he suggested Rally visit a friend she had talked about in Monarch Moon. He thought the remote little town nestled deep in the Ozark Mountains would be a safe place for her to stay for a while. He called Clay and asked him to watch out for her.

Clay had expected someone shy and frightened, but he sensed Rally Chandler to be more capable of taking care of herself than he at first believed. He shook his head when he thought about her forgetting to change her driver's license and trying to cover her embarrassment. She was attractive, with blonde hair and gray-blue eyes that reminded him of soft moonlight on the lake. He suspected her clothes were from upscale Chicago shops. They fit her like the skin on a peach.

He reached under the passenger seat, pulled out a folder, and flipped it open. The picture of the attacker looked like a thousand other thugs. Mean and angry.

The photo of Rally Chandler bore little resemblance to the woman in the Mustang. Fenner had followed her home and shoved his way into her apartment at knife point. He then dragged her into the bedroom, threw her on the bed, and tried to bind her wrists.

A kick to the stomach sent him sprawling. She rolled over, grabbed a Beretta from a drawer in a nightstand and shot him in the shoulder, arm, and stomach. The apartment supervisor called 911 and reported the gunfire.

When the police got there, Fenner lay moaning on the floor in a pool of blood. The victim sat in a corner gripping the gun with both hands, her eyes locked on him.

After the perp went through several surgeries and months of recuperation, her testimony sent him to jail. Before he left the courtroom, he turned toward her and sneered,

"You'll be seeing me again, sweetheart."

Clay closed the folder and slid it back under the seat. He could file it now that he knew what she looked like. That convertible wouldn't be hard to spot.

He was too involved in finding the thieves who were stealing everything that wasn't nailed down to devote a lot of time to watching after her. Sheriff Turner had asked for help from the short-handed Missouri State Highway Patrol to no avail, so all the deputies would work a lot of overtime until they caught the gang.

Clay was acting sheriff until Turner got back from his knee surgery, so he made out the schedule and worked the gaps. That meant seven days a week.

He would have to figure out a way to fulfill his Sunday responsibilities and pray that no emergencies happened there during the week while he was at work. He could only hope and pray the *charming* Miss Chandler was vigilant enough to sense any signs of danger and report them instead of trying to handle them herself.

Chapter 3

Marney's directions were difficult. The town of Monarch Moon was too small for her map, and the GPS quit on her, so Rally pulled off at a scenic overlook. Pea gravel crunched under her bejeweled sandals as she walked to the edge of the bluff, the sound echoing in the quiet morning. A sparkling blue river snaked its way through the valley below. Splotches of autumn red and yellow stained the dark green canvas of trees.

"Hello?" Marney answered the call.

"It's beautiful."

"I know. Where *are* you?"

"I'm at a scenic overlook somewhere off Highway 65. I want to come here later to get some photos."

"We'll have plenty of time and opportunities for photos. What are you doing way over there?"

"You don't give directions well."

"You don't follow directions well."

Both women laughed, then Marney got down to the

business of redirecting.

"When you get close to our road, there's a mom-and-pop fast-food place on the right. Get yourself a soda and wait for me. With your sense of direction, you would never make it the rest of the way on your own."

Thirty minutes later, Rally found the drive-in, bought a fountain 7-Up, turned on the radio, and waited for Marney. She noticed an old, dust-covered truck parked a couple of spaces past her.

A few seconds into a favorite Avril Lavigne song, a Bondo-spotted black pickup came roaring into the parking lot of the Pick-Quick liquor store next door. It came to a screeching halt just a few feet from the door. She reached over, turned down the volume, and watched.

A man wearing a ragged tee shirt and a dirty blue Kansas City Royals cap jumped out. Dark, shaggy hair spilled from under the hat and hung around his face. He rushed into the store and shortly after ran out carrying a big brown bottle.

"That's Jeb Sanders."

The gruff voice startled her. She turned to find steel-gray eyes staring at her from the craggy face of a man who looked to be in his eighties.

"He's stocking up for the weekend ... lives over across the dam." The man nodded over his shoulder. "Fifty kinds of trouble, that one. He hangs out with a wild bunch, thinks he can get by with anything 'cause his cousin's a deputy."

The weathered man wore a straw hat, bib overalls, and a chambray shirt.

"I'm Marney's uncle. She sent me to fetch ya. She got a call she had to mess with, said you'd understand."

"I'm Rally Chandler. I'm pleased to meet you ... Mr. Darnell?" She stuck her hand out.

He hesitated, then shook it. "Call me Will. No sense gettin' all formal. You better just follow me, not too close, though. The road's dusty. Hang back a respectable distance in that rag-top or you'll sure be covered with it. If I can't see you behind me, I'll stop and wait. It ain't far. Just try to keep the dust cloud in sight."

"Oh, I'll raise the top. It won't take a minute." While the top came up, she admired the old pickup that matched its owner's personality.

The truck, faded and dust covered, might have started life a dark blue. She made a mental note to get a picture of the grizzled old man in front of it before she left. Character lines like his photographed well in black and white.

After two forks in the road, Will turned onto an unmarked graveled lane which led to a two-story white frame house. A faded red barn and a couple of sheds sat out behind. Next to the windmill, a stock tank shimmered with water filled to the brim. More photo-ops. She stepped out of the car and stretched.

Will walked around the car and peered into the backseat. "Guess your grips is in the trunk."

"Grips?" She frowned.

"Your suitcases. Now throw me your keys, and I'll haul them in for ya'."

He moved to the rear of the car. "What year is this anyways?"

"It's an eighty-four." Rally reached in for her purse and the back of her hand hit the trunk release. As Will bent over to check out the bluebonnets, the lid flew up and clipped him on the chin.

"Oh, I'm so sorry, Will. Are you hurt?"

He grumbled under his breath as he rubbed his jaw and pulled a suitcase from the trunk. "Next time you do that, young lady, you'd best be a little more cautious about what might be standin' in the way. I was expecting keys tossed over the back, not metal flying up from the bottom." He looked at the contents of the trunk and shook his head.

"That doesn't all go in." She grabbed a denim jacket, threw it over her arm, then pointed out two camera bags and three cases of accessories. "This is photography equipment. It can stay."

"Well, it's a good thing. I don't think that little bedroom she's puttin' you in could hold all that stuff. You must have brought half of New York City with you."

"Ah, I'm not from New York." She brushed road dust from the front of her black silk shirt.

"Well, you're from somewhere east, anyways, that's what Marney said. One place is like any other up there." He was already halfway to the house, even with a noticeable limp.

Rally quickened her pace. "Chicago is northeast."

"A Yankee's a Yankee." The elderly man shook his head.

Rally watched a white-turned-gray ragged handkerchief flop precariously from a hip pocket as he disappeared through the front door.

"I'm not a Yankee. I'm a Texan." She hurried to catch him.

He sat the suitcases inside and held the door open for her. "Come on in. Marney's around here somewhere." His voice boomed into the interior of the house. "Hey, Marney, your Yankee friend is here."

A large living room full of antique furniture spread out in front of her, with an archway to a small dining area on her left. Next to that, she glimpsed a refrigerator and stove. She watched Will wrestle her luggage up a staircase.

Marney stood on the landing. She turned sideways to let Will pass, then rushed down the stairs. "Oh, my gosh, Rally! I can't believe you're here." She hurried across the living room, her arms outstretched.

The clean scent of chamomile soap preceded her. Her still-damp, sun-streaked brown hair, styled in a chin-length bob—much shorter than the long, beautiful locks of their high school years—looked youthful. She wore a simple white cotton blouse and a long red-print skirt that brushed her ankles. Her shoes were well-worn brown leather sandals. Although she looked neat, this was not the fashionista of their earlier years. Somehow, the more natural look suited her.

"You look great, as always." Marney hugged her, then held her at arm's length and looked her over. "A little skinny, though. We'll work on that while you're here. I'm a good cook now, believe it or not. Will taught me." She looked over Rally's shoulder at her uncle, who quietly moved around them and headed back outside.

"Darn good thing, too. That girl couldn't boil an egg, let alone fry one when she first came here." He winked. "I'm goin' out to do some chores. Be back in about an hour. Dinner should be ready by then, if Marney don't spend too much time talkin' and not enough time takin' care of business."

"Dinner's on the finish line," Marney called out as the screen door shut behind him. She then turned to her visitor. "Let's sit down, have a cup of tea, and catch up."

Rally slipped her sandals off and settled into a big easy chair as Marney poured.

"Doesn't he realize you're practically a chef?"

"He does, but he doesn't want to admit it." The women gently touched antique rose patterned cups in a toast, then sipped.

"You have a pleasant trip down?"

"It was great until I ran into the tall, handsome, but exasperating Deputy Woods. You didn't warn me about him."

Marney stared. "You met Clay Woods? He's a nice guy, but he takes his job seriously. He's been through some stuff with a fiancé that ran off without warning a couple of years ago. It's taken him a while to get over that. He's mostly into his job. Likes to keep track of who's new in the county. What did you do to make him stop you?"

"Well, I guess I crowded him off of the road … a little."

She ducked her head, then shifted in the chair. "Oh, and by the way, I'm here for a week, not enough time to get involved in community gossip. Don't need his history. I never thought you would succumb to that."

Marney arched an eyebrow. "Oh, I don't subscribe to ugly gossip, it's just friendly gossip. There's a difference, you know." Frown lines formed on her forehead. "Okay, I get it. I won't bore you with local details, but if I were you, I'd watch the driving. Clay's nice the first time around, but I don't want to be taking a picnic basket to the local jail."

"Well, at least he didn't give me a ticket. That's all I need, a fine to pay the first day I'm here."

"Great start, Rally. I'll have to keep you out of trouble. You haven't changed a bit, have you?"

An awkward silence passed between them. Rally wiped a tear with her thumb as the memory of Fenner lying in a pool of blood flooded her thoughts. "Oh, I've changed. You don't have any idea how much."

Chapter 4

A pile of paperwork covered Clay Woods's desk. While shuffling through the pages, he was more focused on the willowy Miss Chandler than his work. He picked up the clipboard and pulled off the sheet with her name, registration, and license numbers.

I should have issued a warning ticket.

Feet propped on the desk, he scanned the contacts on his cell phone and chose a number.

"Hey, Scott. Thought I'd let you know, your friend Miss Chandler just arrived in Hayes County."

"Thanks, Clay. Fenner would not know to go look for her there. He might head out to Northeast Texas, thinking she might go back home, but she has no family there now."

"Well, she wasn't hard to find. She almost ran me off the road."

Clay heard a chuckle. "That has to be a good story, if you'd like to share."

"She was taking pictures of the scenery along the road and crossed over the center line as I met her going the opposite direction." He twirled a pencil between his fingers.

"In her defense, Clay, she *is* a professional photographer. Most of her work is city stuff. She's never seen all that Ozark beauty before. I'm sure she thinks she's in picture-taking heaven."

"I explained she should do her 'picture-taking' outside a moving vehicle."

"How did she handle that?"

"Okay, although she had an issue with a minor problem over her driver's license."

"Give her a break, Clay. She acts tough on the outside, but she's scared. Hey, did she have the Beretta with her?"

"I didn't have a reason to search her vehicle. I was afraid I might alienate myself right off the bat. If I'm to watch her, I don't want her to run the opposite direction every time she sees me." He lowered his feet to the floor and stared out the window, the memory of her edging into his thoughts.

"She's carrying a load of guilt around and believes she's fallen from grace because she almost killed a man. I've told her she was only protecting herself, but she can't see it that way. She brought the gun but said she would leave it in the glove box."

Clay nodded. "She's staying with her friend, Marney Phillips, and Marney's uncle Will. I drop in there often for coffee, so it's not unusual for me to be around."

"Oh, Marney, eh? New girlfriend?"

"Not at all. Marney's a good friend, but not a girlfriend. We each provided a shoulder to lean on during some rough times, but that's it."

"Okay, friend, if you say so. I'm thinking there may be more friction between you and our pretty Miss Chandler."

"Why do you say that?"

"When she finds out what your weekend job is, she's probably going to run as far away from you as she can get."

Chapter 5

R ally drained a glass of milk, then took the last few bites of blueberry pancakes and homemade sausage patties. She wiped her mouth with a blue-and-white checked napkin and set it down beside her plate. "That was a delicious breakfast. Thank you."

"What would you like to do today besides play catch up?" Marney refilled their coffee mugs from an ancient blue spotted enamel coffee pot.

"Well, there's not much to talk about from my side. Your life is probably far more interesting. Getting some exercise might be a good idea. I can't eat like this while I'm here and expect to go back to Chicago the way I came. Is there a gym nearby?"

"The only gym we have around here is right out there in that barn. Do you want to milk cows, gather eggs, pitch hay from the loft, or shovel manure? Take your pick."

Rally looked at her friend. "You do all that?"

"Nah, I was just joking. We have some chickens and a couple of cows, but Will handles all of that. It keeps him active and makes him feel productive. Losing Aunt Laura nearly killed him. He lost all interest in living, wouldn't eat, couldn't sleep. That's why I moved here. He didn't have anyone left but me, so I had little choice but to come."

Marney smoothed the wrinkles from a blue gingham placemat in front of her, then sat her coffee mug back down. "Of course, I had to lie to him and say I didn't have a place to live. That's the only way he would allow me to move in here. He's super-independent. He thinks he takes care of me."

"That must have been quite a challenge, getting him back into the real world."

"It was hard. I interrupted my life and ruined a relationship to come here to save my uncle."

"Ted?" He was the college boyfriend who went to work with a prestigious law firm in Dallas, the year before Marney was to finish *her* law degree. Rally was to be the maid of honor at their spring wedding.

"Yeah. Seems he found someone else while I was 'wasting myself in Missouri,' I believe is how he put it." Marney stared into her mug.

"Honey, I'm so sorry." Rally reached across the table and touched her friend's hand. "That jerk wasn't worth your time, anyway. You'll find someone better."

"I don't know if I want to. I don't want that kind of disappointment and hurt again. When you're dealing with men, you never know. I doubt that I'll ever trust another." She pushed her chair back from the table and started picking up dishes. "This conversation is getting too serious. I have a surprise for you. Are you game for something different?"

"Sure, why not? I'm on an adventure this week. How should I prepare?"

"You'll want a light wrap, your camera, and a telephoto lense. Oh, and a tripod." She waved her hand in the air. "And whatever other gizmos you use these days, and don't forget your sunglasses. You wanted a working vacation. You're going to get one."

"Great. Sounds fun. Can I at least ask where we're going?"

"Yeah, you can ask, but I don't have to tell you. Just load your stuff. I'll pull the truck around."

Rally pictured Will's old pickup. "Why don't we take my car? My equipment is in the trunk. We won't have to switch it over."

"If you want," Marney shrugged. "But we'll be going over some rough roads. I never take my car over there." She looked out the window at the Mustang. "You think that little thing can take the abuse?"

"Don't let its size fool you. I've taken that car into all kinds of places. It does fine."

Marney packed a lunch and filled a Thermos with coffee and one with iced sweet tea. The sun had not yet warmed the air. The temperature in the hills seemed cooler to Rally than in Chicago. Both women grabbed light jackets and headed for the Mustang. Will met them on his way from the barn.

"Going somewhere?" He had on the same overalls he had worn the day before. Muddy streaks covered the front of one leg.

"What happened to you?" Rally grimaced.

"Got kicked by a cow, well, grazed anyhow. Old Vivian gets a little cantankerous when I milk her. She loves to catch me off guard and lay one on me. I had my hand on her hip, but the witch kicked me anyways." He brushed his pant leg with a rag.

"I'm taking Rally over to Brighton Bridge, to that clear meadow on the other side of the river. I thought she could get some interesting shots there today."

Will sniffed the air and directed his gaze to the cloudless blue sky. "She's a beauty, ain't she? Perfect day for nature watchin'." He turned and looked at Marney. "Anybody reported anything yet?"

"Tom called yesterday. He's seen a few the last couple of days. Said they're right on target, according to that internet site. He's predicting the sky will be full of them today and tomorrow."

"Okay, what's the big secret?" Rally looked from Marney to Will. "You're taking me to see ... flying saucers, maybe?"

"It'd spoil Marney's fun if I told you now." Will grinned, and then absently spit on the ground in front of him. "She wants to see the expression on your face when you get there, if there's anything to see yet. It's hard to tell with this chill in the air. It's windy too. That might make a difference."

He pulled a big red bandana from his hip pocket and wiped his face, then turned to walk down the path to the house. "You girls have fun now. Don't forget about dinner. I'll gather in some of them late green beans and get 'em cookin'."

"There's some pork steak thawing on the drainboard," Marney called out. "Turn it over after a while, okay?"

He waved as he opened the door and walked into the house.

Rally reached into the Mustang. "Let's put the top down. It'll make for a prettier drive."

~ ~ ~ ~

Marney directed Rally across the highway and down another gravel road. They chatted about people they knew from Texas, and who they'd seen or heard from.

"What about that deputy sheriff, the one that stopped me? Clay Woods."

"What do you want to know about him?"

Rally watched a big grin spread across Marney's face.

"No, it's just that he seemed so stiff, so serious. He

acted like he was going to smile at one point, but that didn't last. Does he ever do anything besides sheriff?"

"Like what?"

"Well, does he date anyone?"

"Not now. I told you, he got burned a while back. Why do you ask?"

"Oh, no reason. I thought you might be interested, since that termite dumped you. Maybe you should go for it."

"We're friends. That's all. He comes by to visit Will sometimes, stays for a cup of coffee. He's a nice guy, but no, not at all."

The road narrowed to only a goat trail full of washboard ruts. The little convertible was getting a workout. Rally and Marney jostled around in the front seat while the picnic basket slid across the backseat and the Thermos rolled around on the floor.

"Is this as bad as it gets?" Rally wondered what she'd gotten herself into.

"It gets worse on down. The river sometimes overflows onto the road. Through the years, it's washed the dirt away until in places there's nothing left but bedrock. Nobody seems to be interested in fixing it. We park up here a little way, then walk on down."

"That means you get to help carry my equipment. If I knew what we're looking for, it might give me a better idea of what to take."

"Don't worry. The car will be close enough for you to come back and get whatever else you need. Like Will said, it could be a washout, but there's always the bridge and water to photograph. We may be too early for my surprise. We'll see."

Rally got an occasional glimpse of silver-gray steel through the trees ahead of them. "Is that the bridge over there?"

Marney nodded. "Yeah, that's it. You can park in that wide spot ahead."

Tall oak trees framed both sides of the road. Branches thick with foliage blended to form a canopy above the rock-bottomed lane. Yellow and red-tinged leaves gave the promise of richer color to come. Rally imagined the photographs she could take in this setting. Maybe she would come back later when the trees took on their full fall colors. Her mind painted the forest in shades of gold, russet, red, and orange mixed with the brilliant green of the cedars, all set against the crisp fall sky.

Loaded down with a camera bag slung over one shoulder, an accessory bag over the other, and a tripod clutched under her arm, she chose her steps carefully along the rocky path in front of her. At an abrupt turn in the road, she gasped at the view ahead.

A silver metal bridge spanned a wide river, its mirror image reflected in the quiet water below. The trees, cloudless sky, and clear blue water blended into a watercolor fantasy. A half-dozen mallards paddled below the bridge. The only sounds were the calls of songbirds she had yet to identify and the faint slap of water against rocky banks. She watched bright red cardinals dart between cedar trees along the river.

She sat her equipment down, and for a few moments took in the surrounding beauty. "No artist could paint this. I doubt I can capture it with a camera. It's too perfect."

Marney stooped to set the picnic basket and Thermos on a blanket of late green pasture sprinkled with periwinkle, chicory, and black-eyed Susan.

"I never tire of seeing this. It changes with the seasons, but it's always gorgeous, even in winter. Snow in those cedars reflects on the water. There are always cardinals sitting on the branches. They look like red holiday ornaments. It's prettier than any Christmas card I've seen."

Rally snapped pictures, wandering up and down the bridge, catching a bird in a tree or the ducks walking onto the bank single file, pilfering through the grass for seeds and insects. She noticed a few orange and black butterflies riding the air currents overhead.

"Come back over here, Rally. Take a break and have a sandwich. We have all afternoon if you want." Marney flipped a large red-and-white checked tablecloth into the slight breeze and let it float down onto the grass.

Rally placed a cap over the lens and walked the length of the bridge to the picnic site, then sat down on the cloth opposite Marney and took a chicken salad sandwich out of the basket. Marney poured steaming coffee into a ceramic mug and handed it across.

"Thanks for bringing me here. I haven't seen anything so tranquil in a long time. I could stay here forever."

"No, you couldn't. When Tom Benson lets his cattle in to graze this field, you wouldn't want anything to do with that big old Charolais bull of his. I checked to make sure they weren't here. He has them in a pasture closer to his barn. We're safe today, but you never know. It's always better to check." Marney grinned. "I'd like to have a picture of you running from that old bull."

"I'm sure you would. That's not the least bit funny." Rally turned her attention to another orange butterfly circling the picnic basket. "There's another butterfly. I noticed one earlier. They sure are pretty little things. Look at the black scallops on the wings." She reached for her camera and unsnapped the lens cover, but the butterfly fluttered away before she could aim and shoot.

Marney munched on a cluster of purple grapes as she surveyed the sky and surrounding trees. "There, over there, another one, and over there, above the bridge."

Specks of orange floated in the midday sky. Dozens spread out across the water, some in groups, some alone.

"Look at them." Rally stood, openmouthed. "They're moving across the river in the same direction." More were coming into view. She watched one spiral out of sight on an updraft.

"It's the migration. This is what I wanted you to see." Marney shaded her eyes with a hand and scanned the sky. "The monarchs most times migrate through here in the fall. Sometimes we see a few coming back in the spring, but we see more of them this time of year. The natives say they roost in nearby trees, but I'm not sure where. It's a well-kept secret."

The numbers increased as Rally watched in fascination. She grabbed a camera, removed the lens, and reached into the bag for a telephoto. After a few dozen shots, she removed the camera from the tripod, lay down on her back and started snapping upward.

"I wish some of them would land. Maybe I could get a better close-up."

"Don't count on it. They usually move right on through, but some stop for a snack if whatever's in bloom is to their liking. They enjoy this meadow because of the wildflowers."

A monarch landed on a huge purple aster next to her. Rally rolled up on her elbow, held her breath, and studied the delicate wings as they moved in and out. She lay back down on the grass and watched, spellbound.

"You're so perfect. You are truly a monarch, the queen of butterflies."

Marney whispered next to her ear. "Are you going to take a picture?"

"I'm afraid I'll scare her if I move. I want to watch her for a while."

"It's amazing how they know where to go." Marney slid down next to her. "They've never made the trip before, but their senses direct them to a place where they can procreate and keep their species alive." She rolled onto her back and stared at the sky. "Not so different from us, are they?" She glanced at her friend. "We all have the desire to preserve our race. It's amazing how God put that survival instinct into every single species."

The butterfly's wings pulsed. Rally watched it flutter up and into a distant tree line.

~ ~ ~ ~

For the better part of the afternoon, the women stayed in the meadow. The number of butterflies dwindled.

"What a day." Rally searched the sky for specks of orange. "Shooting like this is so different from shooting for assignments. I love what I do, but there's always pressure on the job. This is relaxing and comfortable. I can't wait to see what I have here. Where can I print some of these?"

"You can do digital prints at Putnam's drugstore."

"We photographers have that instant gratification thing going on, you know. I enjoyed my dark room back in K.C. I still love using film, but it's obsolete now, and—"

Twigs snapped in the line of trees behind them. Rally went on point. A crackle in the underbrush, then the splinter of branches as something—someone—lunged through the woods toward them.

Her first instinct was to grab the Beretta from the camera bag where she used to keep it, but remembered she left it in the Mustang.

A rustle from the timber right behind them sent her spiraling toward Marney, shoving her to the ground. She rolled to a utility bag and withdrew a long-bladed hunting knife. She sprang to her feet, took a throwing stance, ready to let go.

"Rally, no. Don't throw that thing. Look, it's a deer, for Pete's sake." Marney stood and pointed at a large buck, jumping a fence into another pasture. "He's gone."

A few moments passed while Rally composed herself. She looked her friend over. "You okay?"

"Yeah, I think so." Marney brushed herself off, picked debris from her clothes. "What got into you? I've never seen you this jumpy."

"I don't know." She put the knife back in the bag. "Too

long in the city, I guess."

"I remember now how well you could handle a knife. You always out-threw your brothers. Be careful with that thing while you're here." She scanned the camera bags and other equipment. "I hope you don't have a forty-five stashed away somewhere."

"No forty-five, I promise."

Rally repacked her camera bag while Marney loaded the picnic basket and threw the tablecloth over her shoulder. They chatted as they walked back to the car.

Rocks crunched under the tires as Rally backed the car around and headed toward the gravel road. A change in the wind direction blew dust from the road into the car. "Yuck, we're going to be covered. I should have put the top up for the return trip. That air's getting chilly too."

Marney slouched down into the seat and hugged herself. "They've been predicting a cold front for the next few days. Guess it's finally here. It won't be long before we can start using the fireplace. I love this time of year: nice crisp cool days, the smell of wood smoke, pumpkin pies, ham and beans with cornbread, chili, a pot of vegetable beef soup, all that good comfort food."

"You've become a real foodie, haven't you?" Rally stopped the car and raised the convertible top. They put on their jackets, then she eased the car forward over the washboard road.

"That's about all there is to do around here. Down-home cooking is hard to resist. It's not all about the food, though. I love the ping of acorns falling from the oak trees onto metal roofs, the gobble of the wild turkeys in the woods, the—"

"There are wild turkeys here?" Rally slammed her foot onto the brake pedal and threw Marney forward.

"Whoa. You should warn a person before you do that. I'm glad I had my seatbelt fastened. And, yeah, there are turkeys in the woods. We see them around the barn. They come for the corn and grain that Will throws out for the deer and quail."

"You didn't tell me about all that. I want to take pictures."

"Don't get so excited. It's not as if you can go out there and set up your camera and they'll walk right to you. If they see you, they run back into the woods."

"I want to try. Can you show me where they hang out? I could set my camera on the tripod and control it remotely with an app on my phone. I'd love to get pictures of wildlife."

"Okay, we'll get you out there into the wild." Marney turned to look at her friend. "But if a little old deer scares the pants off you, I have little hope of you taking pictures of wildlife." She pointed a finger. "I will not be responsible for anything that happens."

"What could happen?"

"Well, there are other things in the woods, you know."

"Like what?"

"Like snakes, skunks, and bobcats. Last summer they spotted a black bear."

"How about lions and tigers?"

"None of those so far, but you never know."

"I'll take my chances. When can we start?"

"Maybe tomorrow. Depends on the weather. We'll see. I probably shouldn't tell you this, but there are also bald eagles around."

"Bald eagles?" Rally brought the car to a sudden halt for the second time. "I would love to get pictures of bald eagles. Tell me where."

"Take it easy. One thing at a time, okay?" Marney pushed herself back into the seat and adjusted her seat belt.

Twilight was settling into the hills as the Mustang pulled into the driveway. Rally glanced at the glove compartment.

What if Fenner had been in those woods instead of a deer?

Chapter 6

"Those were the best scrambled eggs I've ever eaten. What did you do to them?" Rally scraped crumbs of toast from her plate into the trash and rinsed the dish under the faucet.

"They're brown and fresh. I get them from our laying hens."

"They come in colors?"

"You haven't lived in the city so long you've forgotten about brown eggs, Ral-phene." Marney drawled the name out for emphasis as she wiped the inside of a black iron skillet with a damp paper towel.

Frown lines spread across Rally's forehead. "Don't even start. I never go by that name." She picked up a flour-sack tea towel with a bluebird and the word Tuesday embroidered on the end, twisted it, and popped it on her friend's backside.

"As far as anyone knows, my given name is Rally. I tell people I was a weak, premature baby, but the doctor told my parents I was 'rallying,' and so … that's what they named me."

"Shame on you." Marney took a few steps away. "What's wrong with being named after your dad, anyway?"

"I loved my dad, and I like being called Rally, but Ralphene? Would you want that name?" She shook out the tea towel and started wiping the dishes from the drain rack.

"No thanks. Marney is bad enough. I don't know what my folks were thinking. Sounds more like a name for a dog."

"I like it. Besides, it's unusual. It suits you. You've always been unique. All those far-out hair colors in high school. Then there was the Goth year. Black everything."

"Okay, enough. That's way behind us now. Let's change the subject. I'm afraid, and I mean literally, that you'll be on your own today. I have an appointment at school this morning, and I have grocery shopping and errands this afternoon. You're welcome to come along, but you would probably be bored."

"An appointment at school on Saturday?"

"Yeah. I've been substitute-teaching fourth grade, and a teacher resigned, so they asked me if I would like to apply for the job. Principal Gaines is doing paperwork today and asked me to come while it's quiet with less distraction. Thought I might give it a try. It doesn't look like I'm going to be leaving here for a while."

Rally turned and stared at Marney. "You're not planning on staying here the rest of your life, are you?"

"I don't know. Probably at least until Will's gone. He can't be here alone. I'm all he has. He'd never leave to go somewhere with me. He's too entrenched here."

"You're too smart. You should go back and finish law—" The immediate switch from Marney's happy to somber demeanor sent a message to not go any further.

"Good grief." Rally tapped her watch. "Look at the time. I think I'll go into town, print off some pics from yesterday, and buy another SD card. Then I might scout out some woods for scenic places to set up and shoot. I may run into some of those critters you were talking about." She hung the tea towel across the oven door handle.

"Just be careful, Rally. Make sure you can find your way back. I don't need to waste a bunch of time trying to find you if you're not here in time for supper. These twisty mountainous backroads around here can be confusing to flatlanders."

"I'll be fine." She chuckled. "You worry too much."

"And be careful about trespassing. Some might call Deputy Woods to come get you and take you to jail." Marney smiled.

"I'll be careful. I, for sure, do not want to run into that deputy again, even though he is kind of good looking."

Marney ran a hand across her mouth to suppress a smile. "Of course not."

"I think I'll go where we were yesterday and look around. That's a pretty area." She drained her coffee cup and set it in the sink.

"If you follow the gravel road instead of turning off onto the rock road to the bridge, you'll come out at Paradise Lake. It's beautiful over there. Some areas are over-grown with brush, so a pair of boots might be in order, in case you run across a snake. Be careful and don't get too adventuresome."

"I can take care of myself. I'll probably be back before you are. By the way, where's Will? I haven't seen him all morning."

"He went into town to have some work done on the truck. He goes over to Bill Emory's barbershop and plays checkers every time he gets a chance. I'll check on him before I come home, in case he has to leave the truck and needs a ride."

"I'm going to load up my stuff and take off. See you back here later."

Marney called after her, "Don't forget, tomorrow is Sunday. We'll be going to church."

"Church?" She stopped at the door. "I haven't been to church since I left Kansas City. I think I'll pass."

"No, you won't. Everyone goes to church on Sunday, except for that heathen Jeb and the low life he runs with."

"I didn't bring church clothes. Everything I have with me is casual."

"That's no excuse. I have some of my skinny clothes hanging in your closet. Take your pick."

Frustrated at the idea of having to go to church, Rally let the screen door bang shut behind her.

Chapter 7

Putnam's drugstore was on the south side of the square in a red brick building. The set-up looked like an old-fashioned apothecary with an actual soda fountain. Rally spotted a self-service kiosk to her immediate left when she walked through the door, but there were three people waiting in line. She moved around them to the service desk.

"May I help you?" A dark-haired young woman hurried to the counter. Rally glanced at her nametag. *CeCe.*

"Yes, I'll take one of those SD cards behind you." Rally pointed at a rack against the wall. "Is that the highest storage you have?"

"I'm sorry, it is." She smiled. "You must be planning on taking a lot of pictures."

"I'm a professional photographer, and this area is so beautiful. I can't help myself." Rally handed the clerk her credit card.

"I hope you enjoy your stay."

"I plan to, CeCe. Thank you." She collected her purchase and headed toward the door, but the shiny marble counter of the soda fountain beckoned her.

The clock over the door read 11:55 a.m. She hadn't planned on a lunch break, but a hand-dipped chocolate malt or strawberry soda sounded good.

What the heck? It would be fun to eat whatever I want for a change.

She slid onto a tall stool and looked at herself in the mirrored back of the fountain area and noticed a bit of pink tint on her face, a blush that came from being in the sun the day before. It was refreshing to have some natural color again without makeup.

The mirror reflected the full length of the fountain area. Glistening glassware shot rainbows of light against the side wall. The girl who had helped her at the kiosk hurried behind the counter and slipped into a white lab jacket. She filled a glass with iced water and set it in front of her new customer.

"The menu's on the wall. What will it be?" When the dark-haired girl smiled, her entire face lit up. Deep dimples complemented a tanned, heart-shaped face. Rally liked her. She judged her to be in her late teens or early twenties.

"Okay. What's the lowest calorie treat on that menu?"

"You know, I don't have a clue. I suppose most people who eat what's on there aren't too concerned about the calorie count."

"Then what's the best tasting thing you have?"

"Hmm." She turned and looked at the menu. "My favorite is the butter pecan sundae ... or maybe the strawberry soda." She sighed. "I love strawberry sodas, but I don't indulge much anymore."

"Why not? You certainly don't have a weight problem. You're thin. Diabetic?" After she asked, she realized it was none of her business.

"I'm sorry," Rally said. "I didn't mean to pry."

"Oh, no," the younger woman answered. "You're fine. I need to watch what I eat for, well, maybe a new career. I don't know yet." The smile faded from the girl's face as she stared at the counter and wiped it with a bar rag.

The change did not escape Rally's notice. She pushed away from the bar with both hands, leaned out, and stared at the menu. "Okay then, I'll try a strawberry soda on your recommendation."

"Good choice. You won't be disappointed." The young woman turned and selected a tall soda glass from a group stacked bottoms-up in a triangle. The smile returned as she waved an ice cream scoop over the glass. "Vanilla or strawberry?"

"Give me a scoop of each."

"Excellent."

The girl scooped a huge dip of vanilla ice cream into the glass, then added an equal amount of strawberry and a small dipper of strawberries with syrup. Soda spewed from a spigot and created a frothy pink concoction that was topped off with a mound of whipped cream and a bright red cherry. She inserted a long-handled spoon and a straw into the side of the glass and slid it across the counter.

"Enjoy."

"Thanks. By the way, my name is Rally. I'm visiting here for a few days." She stuck her hand out to the girl.

"Celia. My friends call me CeCe." She wiped her hands on a clean towel and shook the extended hand. "Hope you enjoy your stay."

"I am already. I haven't seen an actual soda fountain in years." Rally sipped from the straw, then spooned out a bite of ice cream. "This is a real treat. You did a great job. It's delicious."

"Thanks. I've had enough practice. My dad owns this place. I work here during the summer and go to college during the school year, but I'm laying out this semester. I need some time to think about what I want to do. My dad isn't happy about it, but he's getting used to the idea, I guess."

Something was bothering the girl. Rally considered telling her that the opportunity to go to college didn't happen for everyone, but she decided against it. She didn't need to get involved with someone else's conflicts. She had enough of her own.

"I'm sure you'll make the right decision. Sometimes it takes a while to find direction." She finished her soda and pushed the glass away, sipped some water, then looked at her watch.

"Oh, it's later than I thought. I need to get on my way." She slid a ten-dollar bill across the counter. "Here. We were talking. I nearly forgot to pay. Keep the change."

"Don't worry. I would have reminded you. I enjoyed talking to you. Come again."

"I might do that." Rally looked back at the kiosk. People were still waiting. "When the line's not so long." She dropped her wallet into her backpack and slid off the stool.

"Tourist season." CeCe smiled. "Thanks for the tip." She picked up the empty glass and wiped the counter.

"You're welcome." Rally waved and walked toward the door at the front of the store.

"Wait!" CeCe beckoned to her.

"If you trust me, I could print photos for you when there's no one here. You could get them later. I wouldn't mind, and it would be fun to see what you captured."

"Of course, I trust you. That's so sweet of you to offer." Rally dropped her backpack on a stool, pulled a SD card from an inside pocket, and placed it on the counter.

"I do it all the time for folks around here. I have free time and I like to keep busy. Dad doesn't mind. He says it's good P.R."

"Print them all then, even if they look bad. I want to see my mistakes."

"No problem. I'll probably have them ready in a couple

of days."

They exchanged cell numbers. Rally walked to the exit.

A young man burst through the door and almost knocked her down. He ignored her, not excusing himself or checking to see if she was okay, but hurried toward the film kiosk and pharmacy area.

"CeCe, where are you? We need to talk. Come on out here."

A man came out of a side office and walked toward the center aisle, blocking the young man's progress.

"CeCe's busy, Doug. You'd best go on. She doesn't want to talk to you, and I don't want you bothering her. You've created enough problems around here. Go on now, please leave."

The man stopped short when he saw Rally standing at the door. He stared at her with the same dark eyes as CeCe's, except these were dull, as though any spark of life was long gone. He was tall, with a muscular build and dark hair sprinkled at the temples with gray. She nodded, opened the door, and walked out.

Curious about what was happening in the store, she sat in her car for a few seconds before engaging the starter.

As she put the Mustang in reverse and backed into the street, the young man named Doug ran from the store and got into an older but pristine red pickup parked behind her in front of the courthouse. The truck backed out and cut off a black SUV, forcing the driver to brake hard while the pickup swerved around and raced through a red light, heading toward the highway that led out of town. The SUV followed in pursuit.

She shook her head, backed out of the parking space and into the street, then headed for the bridge, looking forward to wandering around on the other side of the river and exploring some fresh territory, but she remembered Marney's suggestion to go farther down the main road to the lake.

Chapter 8

Not wanting to put the Mustang through any more
abuse after yesterday's adventure, she pulled over
at a wide spot on the graveled lake road. The walk
would do her good after eating the ice cream soda, along
with Marney's comfort food, for the last few days. With no
idea how far it might be to the lake, she opted to keep her
load light. If the area looked promising, she could always
come back for more equipment later. She might find the
road decent enough to take the car closer if she wanted to
invest more time.

To her surprise, the road was smooth with a gentle
downward slope. The walk proved effortless, and the crisp
fall air was invigorating. Some hardy Queen Anne's lace
bloomed by the side of the road. Wild purple asters and
white daisies spread out along a grassy patch of meadow on
her left. The early frost Marney had talked about at
breakfast seemed to have missed the vegetation here.

She listened for any thrashing about in the woods, alert
for the possibility of another deer plowing through the

underbrush. All she heard was the call of birds and a soft wind combing through the upper branches of the gigantic oak trees on either side of the road.

About a half mile in, the road curved upward. She found herself at the top of a ridge. A yellow barricade cautioned: *Drop off. No lake access.*

Below her, spread out as far as she could see, was Paradise Lake. The dark green of the cedars from the surrounding mountains reflected in the crystal blue water and created a vibrant aquamarine near the shallows, with a dark cobalt in the deeper area toward the middle. Yellow leaves fluttering on the white sycamore along the shoreline added to the contrast.

Perfect!

The mid-afternoon light was ideal from her vantage point. Flares of red and gold here and there in the forest made the scene flawless. She pulled a digital camera from the bag that hung from her left shoulder.

Rally focused and snapped from different angles. When she swept to her extreme right, she caught a glint of sun reflecting off something red in the bottom corner of the viewfinder. She let the camera dangle from the neck strap and stared at the water's edge. A red pickup, several feet from the shore, was sinking, nose first, into the lake. A quick switch to a telephoto lens, set at the highest magnification, enlarged the truck enough for her to suspect it to be the one driven by the young man who had bolted out of the pharmacy earlier. The way he was driving, she wasn't surprised. Shadows filled the cab, making it difficult to see inside.

"Ah, geez. What the heck do I do?" She sat down on a large rock and studied the truck. Maybe someone else would come along and check it out. Perhaps somebody with a truck who could pull it onto shore.

The obvious thing would be to call 911, but then there would be reports that had to be filled out. Maybe the guy was dead in there, or maybe he dumped it for insurance money. Who knew how complicated it could get?

A low moan issued from her throat. She threaded her fingers together, rested her arms on her thighs and lowered her head. Eyes closed tight, she fought the desire to run, to walk away and leave things be, but after a few seconds she stood, put the camera equipment in a pile behind a large oak tree, and scanned the hillside for a path.

The incline, steep and rugged, overgrown with vines and underbrush, looked treacherous. She tried to hang onto tree branches to keep her balance, but a large root, arched above the ground, caused her to trip and fall. "What the … well, this is just great." She struggled to her feet.

Rocks and loose dirt slid under her boots and made her lose her balance again, but she righted herself to a standing position. The embankment was too steep for her to descend any further. She moved backward, hanging onto tree limbs and saplings until she was back at the top of the ridge. She threw her hands up and ran trembling fingers through her hair.

"Why me? I'm here visiting my friend. If I report this, I'll probably have to hang around for hours and answer all kinds of questions. But …"

She reached into her jacket pocket and pulled out her phone. "Hello, I want to report a pickup truck in the lake. Yes, I said in the lake. It's several feet out into the water … sinking."

A half hour later, Rally watched from the top of the hill as a couple of divers hooked a chain to the red truck and motioned for the wrecker to pull it out of the water. She was thankful the whole truck had not submerged. She watched the divers check for a body.

A tall man in a tan uniform and a Stetson got out of a sheriff's car and walked toward the truck. Another deputy, standing by the wrecker, pointed up the ridge in her direction. The new arrival turned back to his car, pulled out a clipboard, and headed up the rugged slope toward her. She watched as he ascended, enjoying that she could look him over without being obvious, but irritated that he made the climb look easy.

"Miss Chandler." He touched the brim of his hat.

Rally nodded. "Deputy Woods. We meet again."

"Yes ma'am. Are you the one who reported that truck sinking down there?" He pointed toward the pickup setting on the lakeshore, water trickling from the open driver-side door.

"Yes, I am. I came here to take some pictures, and I glimpsed it in the viewfinder. When I looked closely, I saw it was a pickup. It looks a lot like the one I saw in town today. A young man was driving it."

"Do you know the young man's name?"

"Well, I was at the drugstore—"

"Putnam's?"

"Yes, it was Putnam's. A young guy came in looking for CeCe, Mr. Putnam's daughter."

The deputy made some notes on the form attached to the clipboard. "Then what happened?"

"Mr. Putnam told him to leave."

His full attention was on her. She fell into the clear blue eyes and lost her concentration.

"Ma'am?"

"Yes?"

"And then what?"

"What?" She shook her head. "Oh, yes, well, I left the store and got into my car. In a minute, the same guy came running out, ran across the street and got into a red pickup, like that one down there, and pulled into the street in front of a black SUV. He was in a hurry."

"So, you don't know the young man's name?"

"Doug. That's what Mr. Putnam called him. That's all I know about him."

"Then what happened?"

"He ran a red light, then headed in this direction on that main street going north- south. The SUV followed him."

"That's all you saw, either there or here?"

"Yes, of course. There wasn't anything else to see after I got here. I saw the truck in the water and called 911."

"Thank you. Ma'am. Appreciate your time. Is there somewhere I can reach you if I have more questions?"

Ma'am? Again? She stiffened, concentrating on a dragonfly gliding across the road. "I'm staying with my friend Marney, at her uncle's place."

"You're staying out at Will Darnell's?"

"Yes, do you know him?"

"Sure. Everybody knows Will. I've beat him a time or two at checkers, but he would never tell you that."

"You don't say." She folded her arms across her chest and stared at her pile of equipment. "I need to go. Marney will think I'm lost. I hadn't planned on being out this long. So, if we're finished here ..."

Deputy Woods lifted his Western-style hat, ran fingers through a shock of wavy caramel brown hair and settled it back down on his head. "Certainly. Thank you for your help. I believe I have your name and phone number from a previous incident."

Rally wrinkled her forehead and stared at the deputy. *Incident? He calls that an incident?*

"You'd better give me your name again, though, just to make sure." He held his pen ready on the clipboard.

"My name is Rally Chandler. I'm from Chicago. I'm here visiting a friend. I take pictures. I have a legal, current driver's license—"

The deputy threw his hand upward in surrender. "Fair enough, Miss Chandler. You take care now." He flashed a big smile that revealed straight white teeth.

"Sure thing, Officer. Glad to be of help."

He tipped the brim of his hat with the clipboard and walked away.

Ah-ha, the clipboard-salute again. Rally watched him make his way back down the hill. He maneuvered with the sureness of a mountain goat, his agility downright disgusting.

The setting sun fired orange rays above the distant mountains and would soon be gone. All creative thoughts at this location were as dry as yesterday's toast. The waterlogged truck and another encounter with the vexing deputy had ruined it for her, taking away her edge.

Walking the incline back to the car was more difficult than she expected. The day's events left her emotionally and physically drained. She stopped twice to catch her breath. As she rested, she reviewed the scene with the deputy sheriff. He was handsome, no doubt. A long sigh escaped her lips. *Another time, another place, maybe.*

She spotted the car at last and began patting her pockets for keys. "I wouldn't have put them in a camera bag. They've got to be in one of these pockets." She dropped the smallest bag to the ground and searched through it, then the larger one.

"I must have left them in the ignition. What a dumb thing to do. That's what I get for being nosy about that incident in town and letting it rattle me. *"*

I've got to get a grip and quit talking to myself. This clean Ozark air is messing with my brain.

Thankfully, there was another key fastened under the hood.

Eager to check the ignition, she opened the unlocked driver's side door.

"I didn't even lock the doors. How stupid is—"

The red-and-white checked tablecloth from the previous day's picnic charged from the backseat into her peripheral vision. A hand reached out from under it and grabbed her wrist.

A male voice commanded, "Don't scream, don't say a word. Do exactly what I tell you. I have a gun."

Chapter 9

Jeb Hendrix slapped his wet fin-covered feet across the rocky shoreline and sat down on the tailgate of a late model Ford truck. He pushed the diver's mask over his head and nodded toward the lake.

"Ain't nobody to be found out there anywhere, Clay. Guess they could have floated on down, but that's not likely. There's no current right there. Carl and I were diving over on the other side of that bluff all mornin'. We didn't hear or see nothing. We were about to move on closer to home when we got the call and come runnin'. I don't think anybody was in that truck, to be honest with ya."

Deputy Woods studied the dripping tailgate and bumper of the red vehicle. "The truck likely went in on its own. The registration is in Doug Palmer's name. He took good care of that truck. The chances are low that he meant to run it into the lake. He spent more money on it than he ever would a girl."

A smudge of black on the truck's bumper caught his attention. He bent over and rubbed across it with his thumb. "That gal on the cliff know anything?" Jeb began peeling off the wetsuit and swim trunks.

"Good grief, Jeb. Get behind a tree or something. I can't have you stark naked out here in broad daylight. What if the press comes out here?"

"Take it easy, Deputy. Carl brought this here truck around with my clothes right there in the bed, see?" He pulled jeans, underwear, and a T-shirt across the tailgate and began dressing. "That gal the one that's staying over at Will's?"

"Yeah, how'd you know?"

"Everybody knows. Ain't nobody that good lookin' from around here." Jeb grinned at the deputy and waggled thick black eyebrows up and down. "Lessen it's Marney."

"You noticed that, huh?"

"And you didn't?"

"Yeah, I noticed. But I'm working. I don't mix women with work."

"Says who? I've seen your cruiser parked out there at Will's house more than once. You didn't go out there to see Will, either. You were after some of Marney's comfort food." The dark unibrow arched across his forehead like a caterpillar in its winter coat.

"Look, Jeb. We might be cousins, but that doesn't allow you to stick your nose in my business. There was never anything going on between Marney and me. I went by for coffee a few times, mostly to visit when I was already in the neighborhood. I *do* get a break now and then." His shoulders stiffened.

"Okay, if you say so, cuz." The corner of Jeb's upper lip curled into a guarded grin.

"Marney's still hung up on some guy she was engaged to, and I told her about, well, we had some things in common. She's a nice gal. When she gets over that guy, she'll be a good catch for someone." The deputy leaned over the grassy area and stared at something on the ground. "Are you thinking about seeing her yourself, Jeb?"

"Maybe, maybe not. I've got me a gal over toward Forsyth, you know. She's far enough away she don't keep her nose in my business, but close enough to make the trip there and back on a quarter tank. That's just the way I like it."

Jeb grabbed his T-shirt, rubbed it over dark, shaggy, wet hair in need of a serious cut. His build was shorter, less muscular than the deputy, but constant exercise in holding his breath had developed impressive chest muscles. He could stay underwater, without the use of any equipment, longer than anyone else in the diving club. He liked to brag about it to whoever would listen. That, and his freaky way of controlling his eyebrows, were his only claims to fame. He made the most of them.

"Maybe I'll slide on over by Will's sometime and see if I can get me a cup of coffee with Miss Marney." He checked himself out in the side window, slicked his damp hair back from his forehead, and smiled at his reflection.

Clay squatted and examined a tire track on a patch of muddy grass, then pulled his phone from his pocket and took a picture. He tried to concentrate on the task at hand, but a little blue convertible, perfectly manicured fingernails, and eyes the color of winter-gray sky kept popping into his head.

Jeb interrupted his thoughts. "Hey, since that gal's staying with Marney, maybe we can go call on them together."

"Sorry, bud. I've got my hands full right now." He turned to look at his cousin. "You go right on over there and spread your charm around."

"Well, at least it's good to see you still have a sense of humor. I've been worried about you lately. You haven't been much fun, you know. I was gonna ask if you wanted to go huntin' later, but I was half afraid you'd pull that gun and shoot off one of my ears."

"I haven't been that bad, have I?"

"Pretty bad. Folks are talkin'. You've got half the county scared to death to make a U-turn, or leave a skid mark anywhere, 'fraid you'll track 'em down and ticket 'em."

"Yeah, well, I've had a lot on my plate lately. Lots of orneriness going on around here, and with the sheriff out with knee surgery, makes us a man short with twice as much work."

"Still haven't found out who's been breakin' and enterin'?"

"Nope." Clay stood straight and stretched his back. He made more notes on the clipboard. "We'll find them, though. We always do. It's just a matter of time."

Jeb pulled his ball cap down over his forehead, tucked his chin against his chest, and turned his back.

Clay headed toward the patrol car, then turned and looked at his cousin. "If you're serious about heading over to Will's, I think I might need to talk to Miss Rally again. They might have a couple extra cups of coffee brewed. I'll finish here and meet you there."

Jeb slipped on his work boots and headed for his truck. "Okay, cuz. I'll see you at Will's then." He slid into the driver's seat, started the engine, and spun the tires, throwing loose gravel.

Chapter 10

Rally gripped the wheel with both hands and tried to make out the faded tracks on the abandoned road. She could feel the hot breath of the man sitting on the edge of the seat right behind her. Cold metal pushed into the back of her neck. Her heart was beating double-time as she followed his directions, taking them deeper and deeper into the forest surrounding the lake.

A thick growth of oak and cedars blocked out the fading sunlight. Visibility was dim. Her captor would not allow her to turn on the headlights. The little Mustang bounced around on the uneven ground.

"I don't know how much longer I can stay on this path. I can hardly see."

"It's not much farther. K-keep going until I say."

She tried to get a glimpse of the man in the rearview mirror, but the dark interior kept him in shadows. One thing she knew for sure. That was not Fenner's snarly voice. This one was too young, too scared.

"Keep your e-eyes looking straight through the windshield. You don't need to see anything back here."

"What do you want from me? I don't know who you are. I won't be able to tell anyone. Why don't you get out and walk on to where you want to go? I'll try to find my way out of here, then I'll go back to Chicago. I won't tell anyone we've even met."

"Sure, you will. You'll go tell them exactly where you last saw me, and they'll have bloodhounds and helicopters all over the place."

She raised an eyebrow. "Don't you think that's a little dramatic?"

"That's what they do, isn't it?"

"How would I know?" She shifted in the seat enough to get a quick glimpse into the backseat. All she could see was a dark shirt.

"Nobody's ever chased me like that," she spoke over her shoulder. "I've never broken the law, well, except for a couple of traffic tickets."

"You still have a license? Your driving is terrible."

"I'm not your chauffeur, for Pete's sake. You kidnapped me, remember?"

"Don't you … don't you get smart now. Remember, I've got a gun."

She glanced at the camera bag nestled in the passenger seat. After the last scare with Marney, she carried her gun in the bag within easy reach, but any attempt to unzip the cover and reach inside could be disastrous, both short and long term. He could shoot her the instant she made the move, even if she was fast. Worse yet, she could hurt another human being if she succeeded.

The thought of experiencing a trauma like the one with Fenner was unbearable to her. She might never recover.

Her dim reflection in the rearview mirror caught her attention, but her captor was not visible.

Slow down, Rally. You know guns. Something about this

doesn't feel right.

"What kind of gun is that?"

"That's nothin' you need to know. It's just a gun, any gun. What difference does it make?"

"It's just that the bore seems small. Can't be much of a gun if you ask me."

"Well, I didn't ask you, and I don't know nothin' about the bore of this gun. It's a gun, and it has bullets. That's all you need to know."

She pushed down on the accelerator a bit at a time, hoping he wouldn't notice. If she could keep him distracted, she might have a chance. He had control of the gun, but she controlled Blue. Size and force meant everything right now.

"Well, I know all about bore. That feels like something left over from your daddy's childhood toy box. You sure it doesn't require caps?"

The pressure on her neck increased.

"Look, lady. I don't need your opinion on anything. Maybe instead of me getting out, I'll kick you out and take your car. By the time you walk back to the highway, I'll be way gone."

Rally rose off her seat, clenched her teeth, and slammed her foot on the brake. She heard a soft thud when his head hit the back of her seat. His right arm extended into her field of vision. As the car shuddered to a stop, she whipped around, grabbed his arm with both hands, and jerked it hard, hoping to dislodge the gun. Instead, a small flashlight, minus the bulb frame, bounced across the camera bag and onto the floor.

"Ouch! What are you trying to do, kill us?"

She turned on the overhead light and twisted around to look her captor in the face.

"You! It's you! You kidnapped me! Not to mention you drove your truck into the lake and nearly caused a collision with that black SUV in town this afternoon. Are you insane?"

A knot blossomed on Doug Palmer's forehead as he pulled his arm from Rally's grasp.

"That's not so. I didn't drive my own truck into the lake. That truck is my most prized possession. I take better care of it than I do myself."

Rally looked at his scraggly blond hair and disheveled appearance. "That's obvious."

"Second, I didn't mean to kidnap you. Your car was the first place I could find to hide. The car that was behind me in town? The driver might be the one who put my truck in the lake, at least that's what I think."

"This is confusing." She rubbed the indentation in the flesh of her neck.

"Look, there's an old, abandoned cabin here. I come to fish and hunt sometimes. It's remote and hard to get to and a safe place to hang out for a while."

Rally looked out at the night settling around her. If she tried to leave by herself, she doubted she would get any directions from him. Even if she could get a signal in this wilderness, she wouldn't know where to tell Marney to come looking for her.

She sighed. "I've come this far. You look harmless without a flashlight in your hand. Guess I can go a little farther, but just so you know, my little Mustang is as precious to me as your truck is to you."

The cabin, hidden from the rest of the world by an overgrowth of brush, sat in a dense forest of oak and cedars. Doug fetched a machete from the cabin to slash through some of the growth so Rally could move the car forward. She felt Doug was harmless, but the fact he now had a big knife in his possession made her a little apprehensive. She watched him try to cover the Mustang with cedar boughs.

"Enough. There better not be one new scratch on Blue when we leave here, or you get to pay for a paint job.

Driving through all that brush was nearly impossible, and it's dark. Don't you think this might be overkill?"

"You can never be too careful. I don't know for sure who I'm hiding from or why. Until I do, I'm not taking any chances."

The inside of the cabin was clean. She had expected a lot of dust and cobwebs.

"You've been here more often than you led me to believe. It's that, or someone else cleaned it. I don't think you would have kept it this spotless." She gave his disheveled look another once over.

"CeCe, she did it. We used to come here to spend time together. Her daddy really didn't like her hanging out with me, so she had to sneak around. We needed somewhere to meet. I knew about this cabin, knew it wasn't used much. She cleaned it up. We came here ..."

"The two of you used to come here?" Rally looked around the cabin.

"Yeah, before she met Larkin Biggs."

"Who's Larkin Biggs?"

"He's some big-time hotshot from back east, came in here and claimed to be a land developer, wants to buy land around the lake. He went by the drugstore one day, saw CeCe, told her she's model material and that was all it took. She's wrapped around his finger."

He paced the oak flooring as he talked.

"She even dropped out of college this semester because he told her she should go to school to be a model. Said he would pay for it. Her dad thought she was staying out because of me, that I was trying to talk her into marrying me. That's not so. I was trying to be her friend. He would never let me explain and CeCe wouldn't tell him, afraid he would run that land developer off."

"That doesn't explain Biggs chasing you, if that's who it was, and your truck being in the lake." Rally sat down in an upholstered chair, the fabric faded and worn.

"Beats me. Biggs must think I might talk CeCe into changing her mind, but I didn't think I was enough of a threat that he would try to sink me and my truck in the lake."

"Wait a minute." She straightened. "You were in the truck when it went into the lake?"

"Yeah, I came down to the lake to cool off and think, then fell asleep. Someone must have knocked me on the head. I've got a sore place right here." He rubbed his crown. "Along with the new one you gave me on the forehead. When I woke up, there was water seeping into the truck and running across my legs, so I rolled down the window and squirmed out of there."

"That guy must be a poor loser. I can't imagine anyone doing something that drastic over a woman, but it happens. That's extreme ... and cowardly."

He paced the floor, then turned to face Rally. "Look, I'm sorry for kidnapping you and your car. I was desperate. All I know is somebody is trying to kill me. What would you do?"

Chapter 11

C lay Woods drained the last swallow of coffee and set the mug down on the table.

"So, the last time you saw Ms. Chandler was early this morning?"

"Rally, her name is Rally. Ms. Chandler sounds old." Marney pulled a faded brown cardigan sweater close around her, then took a sip from her coffee mug.

Jeb refilled his cup from the blue enamel carafe setting in front of Marney.

"You know, me and the deputy here, we was going to come over and call on you and Ms. ah, Rally. Didn't expect we would come under these circumstances. I'm sure she's okay, now don't you worry." Jeb reached across the table and patted Marney's hand.

"She'll probably find her way back here pretty soon."

Marney drew her arm back, flicked his hand with her fingernail, and looked down her nose at the breath-holding champion.

"Don't patronize me. I'm not an idiot. I get disoriented in those woods after dark, and I know them like the back of my hand. Rally is a stranger here. She doesn't have a clue how to survive in the woods."

The deputy filled his cup from the carafe. "I saw her early this afternoon. She reported an incident over at the lake. I answered the call and got her statement. She must have left right after I talked to her. When I started back up on the bluff to ask a couple more questions, she was gone. I figured she came back over here. Thought I'd catch up with her later."

He pushed his chair away from the table and turned sideways to look through the window toward the barn.

"You say Will took his bloodhound out to look for her?"

Marney stood at the sink, poured water for a second pot of coffee.

"Well, yeah, for what good that will do. Otis is getting too old to go out like that. Will most likely is going to wind up carrying him back here. I don't know what he was thinking, dragging that poor old thing out through the woods in the middle of the night. They've been gone for several hours. We'll probably have to go looking for them when it gets daylight."

Jeb roared with laughter, which brought on a series of loud snorts. Everyone knew he was prone toward them, but it came as a shock every time. Marney and Clay stared at him. Jeb sobered, then turned to Clay and lowered his voice.

"A picture flashed through my head of those two old varmints out there trying to find that girl. That old hound probably flopped down under the first tree he found and fell asleep. Will's crazy to think that dogs got any scenting left in him." He slapped a hand over his mouth to cover his snickering.

Marney reached across the table and punched Jeb's shoulder with her fist. "Will loves that dog. Don't you be talking mean about either of them. He won't give up on Otis until one of them drops dead. It's anybody's guess which one it will be. That dog is probably as old as Will."

"I didn't mean anything bad, Marney." Jeb sobered like a scolded child. "I thought it would be a funny sight, that's all."

"Well, amuse yourself some other way than insulting Will and his hound."

Clay interrupted the banter. "Okay, you two. Let's try to keep things civil." He directed his attention to Jeb. "That thought could have gone unsaid."

Jeb scowled. "Well, she don't need to be so touchy. I was just jokin'."

"It's just a short time until sunrise. I'll report Ms., uh, Rally missing. We can get a search party together before daybreak, but there's no sense sending anyone into those dense woods in the pitch-black tonight. Will knows how to survive. How about Rally?"

"Her family camped a lot. She can take care of herself. It's just that she's not used to the terrain here."

"I'm sure she's alright, Marney. Maybe a little scared, but she seems like an intelligent woman. She'll figure it out. I'll call you first thing to see if she made it home before I organize a search. If she turns up in the meantime, would you give me a call?"

"Sure. I'll call you. I'd feel a lot better if Will and Otis would come home. They're both too old to be out there in those woods at night. Worse than that, Will took his shotgun. He's apt to shoot at anything that moves, then worry about identifying it later. Rally would be a lot safer without Will and Otis in the mix."

Clay rubbed his forehead and stared at the floor. "That isn't good news. Will's an excellent shot, but if he gets disoriented, he might be dangerous."

"He gave Otis some of Rally's belongings to sniff. If that old hound can still smell anything, he might at least identify her before Will starts shooting."

Jeb drained his coffee cup, glanced at Marney, then at Clay. A sheepish grin crossed his face. "Think I should hang around here with Miss Marney in case Will comes back injured from shooting himself?"

Marney grabbed Jeb's empty coffee cup and carried it to the sink. "You're done here. I can take care of myself, thank you. Will's not so old he's going to shoot himself. And if he did, I could probably handle it better than you."

Clay stood. "You come with me, Jeb. You can help me get some men together for the search first thing in the morning. I'll take you home now, so you can get a couple hours of sleep before sunup. I'm going to catch a few winks myself." He yawned.

"You'll let me know, Marney?"

"Sure. I won't be able to sleep until Will gets back, but I'll have coffee ready when you all get here. I'm no good at sitting and waiting, so I'll go with you in the morning."

"Suit yourself. You're as good a hunter as any man around. We can use you. I'll see you about daybreak."

"Great, and thanks, Clay. I know Rally may have pushed a few buttons, but she's a nice girl."

"No problem. It's my job, pushed buttons included. Goodnight."

Jeb hesitated in the doorway. "You're sure you don't want—"

"No Jeb, I don't want." She shut the door, pushing him out.

He shrugged and followed the deputy to the car. "Want me to drive?"

"You know I can't let you drive a patrol car. Don't even think about it." Clay settled into the driver's seat and started the engine.

"I was just thinking about you. Trying to give you a break is all. You've had a busy day."

"Yeah, sure you were." Clay frowned. "Seems kind of

funny that Doug's pickup went into the lake and then Rally disappeared on the same day. Then the developer called and said Doug pulled out in front of him and sped through town. Miss Chandler saw that happen, although she didn't know who was driving the SUV. It all seems mighty strange."

"Well, you know what they say about a full moon, and this one's a Monarch Moon." Jeb craned his neck through the open passenger window. "That makes it twice as bad."

"You don't believe that old wives' tale, do you?" Clay peered through the upper windshield, trying to glimpse the harvest luminary.

"I don't know. I've always heard that when the monarchs migrate, and there's a full moon, watch out. Strange things happen."

"Strange things happen when there isn't a Monarch Moon. It's a coincidence, nothing more. People like to feed the story a little, so they wait for things to happen. Don't you feed into it. I don't want a bunch of people spooked. That's all I need."

Jeb stretched his legs and settled back into the seat. "I'm kind of half-and-half. There might be some scientific explanation, like that butterfly effect thing they talk about. You know that thing about if the butterfly goes on one side of the tree instead of the other, it can change the whole echosystem."

"Echosystem?"

"That's what I said, 'echosystem.'" Jeb wiggled his eyebrows up and down, readjusted his legs and settled his ball cap down over his eyes. "I saw it on Nat Geo."

"It has nothing to do with echoes. You mean ecosystem, how living things relate to their environment."

Jeb sat for a moment. "That changes my whole concept of that. I thought it had something to do with how echoes bounce around. I wondered how a butterfly had anything to do with that. Life is strange, huh Clay?"

"I wouldn't worry about it too much if I were you. It's way beyond anything you need to be thinking about, and I've got enough right here and now, butterflies or no butterflies."

Clay slowed the cruiser and followed the shoreline of the lake to cross over the dam. The water looked peaceful with the moonlight creating silvery sparks on the slow-moving waves. He turned down a gravel driveway and drove through the entrance to Happy Haven Trailer Court, then pulled in next to the third trailer on the right side of the road.

"Here you are, Jeb. I'll see you in a couple of hours. Try to catch a few zees. I'll call you when I'm leaving my house."

"Sure. See you then. Hope that gal shows. I hate getting up before daylight. That's why I like workin' nights." Jeb opened the car door, then turned to look at Clay. "I got to look for a job soon."

Clay watched Jeb saunter toward his trailer. He thought of an old saying he'd heard years ago.

"Jobs are hardest to find after dark, aren't they, Jeb?"

He backed the cruiser around and headed out of the park.

Chapter 12

Rally paced the floor with her hands laced behind her head. "You should probably ask someone else that question."

"What question?" Doug stood at the sink and turned on the cold-water faucet.

"The one about what I would do if somebody tried to kill me."

"Sure." He bent down and banged on the reluctant spigot with his fist. "Like you would have a clue."

"Hmm. Yeah, you wouldn't think that, huh?" She watched with interest as water sputtered from the faucet, then sprang to life, spewing a wide stream over Doug's face and shirt.

"Hey!" He grabbed a towel from a nail over the sink.

She couldn't stop laughing. "I kinda saw that coming."

"Thanks for the warning. I thought a cup of coffee might be nice. I know there's some Folgers in the cabinet." He mopped his hair and the front of his shirt with the towel.

"And how were you going to brew it? Does that stove

have fuel?" She pointed to an ancient gas range sitting next to the sink.

He scratched his head, looked at the stove. "I think CeCe and I drained the propane tank last winter when we were here. I could throw some wood into the fireplace. It wouldn't take but a minute to get it going."

"I don't plan on being here long enough to get a fire going and make coffee. I'm not feeling too friendly right now, so a chummy cup of coffee is out of the question. Besides, aren't you afraid the smoke might raise suspicion?" She wiggled her fingers in front of his face. "Your land developer friend could still stalk you."

"I get it. You're having fun with me, or is it revenge for the trip through the woods? I know you think I'm paranoid, but I'm sure that guy is after me. This is the second time he screwed me up. He got me fired from my job a couple of weeks ago." Doug slammed the towel into the sink.

"You work?" She raised her eyebrows.

"Yeah, I work." He squinted and stared at her. "I had a good job. I was an EMT for the ambulance service over at Hayes."

"Hayes?"

"Hayes Memorial Hospital. It's the only one within fifty miles. It's small, but it stays busy even without the tourists and lake traffic in the summer." He straightened and pushed out his chest. "I worked on lots of emergencies. We were always on the roll."

"How do you know it was Biggs that got you fired?"

"My boss told me, well, more-or-less. He said he got a call from personnel, that some guy called in and said he saw me driving erratically in the ambulance, that I nearly mowed down an old lady in a crosswalk, and that I was speeding and ran a red light. Said he followed me. Those were all lies." Doug clenched his fists as his jaw muscles tightened.

"Well, I could vouch for some of that reckless driving

on your part myself. You sure zoomed out of that parking space after you left the pharmacy. What was that all about?"

Rally winced at his hurt expression. "I'm sorry. I'm being too nosy, although after being kidnapped, I think I should be able to ask all the questions I want."

"Nah, it's okay. I told you. CeCe's dad doesn't like me. He thinks I'm a bad influence, and that it's my fault she's not going back to school this semester. She won't tell him about Biggs."

"I'm hoping CeCe sees through him before he ruins her life. Has she said anything about him wanting her to leave town with him?"

"Well, I don't see many modeling opportunities around here now, do you? That's all she talked about when she was still seeing me. Getting away from here and going to a big city." He dropped his head and stared at his hands. "It hurt me to hear that."

Rally walked around the cabin, rubbed her hand across the polished old logs, and examined the chink between them.

Whoever lived here before took good care of the place.

"We need to get you home. You can give me directions from your place back over to Will's farm. Where do you live from here?"

He sat down on the edge of the bed and stared at the fireplace. "Across the dam." He hesitated a moment, then looked up at Rally.

"You know, there is one other thing. I hadn't even thought of it until now. My grandma owns the trailer park where I live. Biggs was trying to buy it last month. Grandma was thinking about selling it to him, but he wasn't offering enough. I kind of talked her out of it. I mentioned several reasons she shouldn't. Like, where would she live? He wasn't offering her enough to buy another place and support herself for the rest of her life.

The trailer park is a source of income every month and I would do the maintenance. I told her I would help her run it when she got too old. He might have been upset about that."

"Why would he want your grandmother's trailer park?"

"Because it adjoins the property that he's trying to buy for his housing development."

"And where is that?"

"Forty acres of prime property on the west side of the lake. It belonged to CeCe's grandmother. It will belong to CeCe when she turns twenty-one. Right now, her dad is the executor of the estate."

"Bingo! Did it not occur to you that might be the reason Biggs is so interested in CeCe? If he can control her, he can control the estate when she comes of age. How old is she now?"

"Her twenty-first birthday is in a couple of months. I didn't even give that a thought." His face brightened. "You're pretty smart."

"Well, you meet lots of smooth talkers living in a city. I've seen it before."

"CeCe's been lonely. She told me I was the only thing that kept her going ... until she took up with that other guy. He's way too old for her. Did I tell you that?"

"How old is he?"

"I don't know for sure, but I would guess he's around forty."

"Hmm." Rally stared at the wall and rubbed her chin. "So, CeCe is going to have property? What about money?"

"Oh yeah, there's money. Her grandmother was Elinor Pryor Hayes. Elmer Hayes, CeCe's grandfather, donated the money to build the hospital. Their family was one of the first to settle this area, descendants of Eli Hayes, Monarch Moon's founder." He paced a square on the old linoleum, while tapping a finger on his chin.

"The family started the first mercantile store in the

county. They passed it down until the big box store came in and took all their business. It was time for CeCe's granddaddy to retire, anyway. CeCe said she thought he was relieved, even though it broke his heart to leave the business." His voice cracked. "CeCe and I hate that the old store building is now a sub shop."

Rally opened the door and looked out. "That adds more suspicion. I'll admit that, but you're not scaring me anymore, so I think we should get out of here and let people know we're both okay. I'm sure Marney will think I've lost myself in the woods, trying to take pictures of wild animals. She's probably got a search party out after me. You should go talk to the law, so they can quit dragging the lake." She patted his shoulder.

"It'll be okay." He shrugged. "They won't have divers out until morning."

"Divers were there when that deputy sheriff was talking to me. It looked like they were getting ready to leave, though. What about your grandmother? Won't they be checking with her to see if she's seen you? It will scare her to death."

"Oh, my gosh, you're right." He patted his pockets. "Cell service is spotty here. We'd better find our way out. It's really dark, even with a full moon."

Rally crossed her arms and raised her eyebrows. "You don't have to feign innocence with me, sir. I'm sure you found your way out of here with CeCe when it was this dark."

His face turned red as he pushed unruly strands of hair away from his eyes. "We never stayed this late. She had a curfew, even after she turned eighteen. Her dad always wanted to know she was home safe when he worked late.

"You don't have to explain anything to me, Doug."

"Oh no, it's okay. We never … CeCe was a good girl, ma'am. We talked about a lot of things, mostly about what we would do after she got out of college, and I finished nursing school … about our dreams."

"You're in nursing school?"

"No. That's another reason I'm so mad at that guy." He clenched his fists again and tapped them against his outer thighs. "I applied for a scholarship from the hospital. They do tuition reimbursement but, since I lost my job, that's gone, too."

"I would guess you're in his way. Maybe he's giving you more credit than you deserve. I don't see how you could hurt him much, but I suppose he might think you can." She pulled the curtain away from the window and peered out into the darkness. "Let's go. We'll talk about this on the way back, okay?"

"Yeah." He relaxed his hands. "Hey, thanks for being so nice about everything. I didn't know what else to do. It was a gut reaction. Sorry I scared you."

"It's okay, Doug." She laid a hand on his shoulder. "But we need to concentrate on getting home right now."

"I'll get the flashlight from the kitchen." He turned to go. "Then I'll try to turn the car around. I hope I can get it out of that brush pile."

She shook her head and pushed an index finger into his chest. "Oh, no. I'll do the driving, thank you. My car had better not have one scratch on it. I have kept it in mint condition. Blue is my best friend right now."

"At least you still have a car. There's no telling what that trip into the lake did to my truck. That's another thing he's done to me, ruined my truck. You talk about mint condition. My truck is … was … awesome." He shook his head and walked to the door.

Rally backed the car down the road as Doug walked behind her and motioned with the flashlight in the direction she should steer. As soon as she cleared the brush piles, he made a circle of light with the flashlight, signaling her to turn the car around. She stopped and Doug crawled into the passenger seat.

"Would it be a stretch of the imagination to assume I can trust you to get us back on the right road?"

"You don't trust me yet, after all we've been through together?" He sneaked a quick look at her and grinned.

"You mean what I've been through, don't you?" She nailed him with her eyes. "If you remember, I didn't come here willingly. This wasn't my idea of a picnic. You have food with those."

"I can't believe you feel that way. I spilled my guts to you and thought you understood, thought you were on my side." He settled into the seat and clicked the seatbelt.

"Look, Doug." She shook her head. "I don't have a side. I have no interest here except for Marney and her uncle. You've had some bad luck. That's tough, but I'm not getting involved. I'm going back to my own problems in a few days." She turned to look at him. "Understand?"

"Well, good for you." He stiffened and glared back at her. "You can take off and forget it. It's not that easy for me. I live here and have something invested. I want nothing from you, just a little understanding, that's all. You seemed interested while we were in the cabin."

"Ah, Doug," she reached over and patted his knee. "When I figured out you weren't going to kill me, steal my car, and take my cameras and hock them, it brought me back to my senses. I wasn't too sure back there what you might be capable of. Although, I did finally figure out you are a bit of a wimp."

He bristled, leaned against the car door, and pulled his legs out of her reach.

"It was dumb of you to leave the keys in your car and not check it out before you crawled in. It's not my fault you're a dumb blonde. Ah, maybe a better choice of words would be careless blonde."

"I'll take it. Better to be known as a careless blonde than a dumb blonde. I appreciate your kindness in reconsidering that statement."

"Well, you called me a wimp."

"Are we in a spitting contest here or what? Give it up. I can beat you at any games you want to play. I've had lots of experience with that."

"You've met some jerks, haven't you?"

"Why do you think that?" She felt him watching her.

"You're tough."

"Sometimes you have to be." A memory of Fenner came roaring back, and she felt a tear slide down her cheek.

~ ~ ~ ~

As the car edged out of the maze of dense woods and onto the gravel road, Rally stared at the misty silhouette of hills set against a yellow and pink eastern sky.

"Look, the sun's coming up. Marney must be frantic. She probably thinks I'm wandering around in the woods somewhere. I hate that I'm causing her to worry. I should have stayed home and waited until she could go out with me. None of this would have happened if I hadn't been so headstrong."

"It's my fault." Doug shifted in his seat to look at Rally. "If I hadn't abducted you, you'd be home safe and sound. I'm sorry. You're a nice gal. I should have walked home, but I didn't know who was after me and what they might have done if they found me. If somebody tried to drown me, I didn't want to be defenseless, walking down a road without as much as a tire iron for protection."

"You should talk to the deputy sheriff and tell him what's happened to you. Maybe he can figure something out. I'm not a detective. I have no experience in solving mysteries ... or an attempted drowning. Leave it to the experts."

"But what do you think?"

Rally chewed her bottom lip and kept her eyes on the road. She had to be careful with her response. She drew in a deep breath, then exhaled.

"I'm not sure. The land developer may want you out of the way so he can make off with CeCe, but do you think Mr. Putnam dislikes you so much that he would do something like that?"

"I don't know. He's been a different person since his wife died. He sure doesn't like me going around CeCe. I wish I could tell him she's in more danger than he realizes with Biggs. He hasn't a clue that she's hanging out with him."

"I don't think you'll get the chance to discuss it. The way he acted yesterday in the pharmacy, you're the last person with whom he wants to discuss his daughter."

"Would you go talk to him?"

"Me?" She turned and looked at her passenger. "I told you, I don't want to be involved. I don't know these people. Who's going to listen to me?"

"Sometimes an outsider can get through when someone close can't. Would you try?"

Deep down, she knew it to be the right thing to do. "CeCe seems like a nice girl. She reminds me of myself. I dreamed of going to the city and being a famous photographer."

"And you did." Doug pointed to the camera equipment in the backseat.

"I did it the hard way." She stared through the windshield. "I listened to a neighbor's visiting cousin talk about all the prosperity in Kansas City. He said there were unbelievable job opportunities, that they were grabbing people off the street and hiring them for big wages." She swallowed. "I broke my family's heart by going there instead of finishing college, but he said K.C. had a fabulous art school with a great photography program. I had visions of my work being shown in galleries." She sighed.

"All I found in Kansas City was high rent and a tough life trying to make a living doing freelance photography and working part time. I didn't want to go back home to Texas and admit defeat. I felt so alone."

"Do you want CeCe to make the same mistake?" The pain in Doug's voice was palpable.

"No. I don't want her to be disillusioned like I was."

He stretched the seatbelt and turned toward her. "Sounds like a bummer."

"Well, let's just say he wasn't in management like he told me, and he didn't turn out to be someone I wanted to be around."

"I know I'm being nosy—"

"Yeah, you are being nosy," Rally said. "But what?"

"But how did you end up in Chicago?" Doug asked.

"Hmm. I don't know why I'm telling you all this. If you share any of it, I may have to come back and hunt you down."

Doug ran a fist across his mouth. "Zipped shut."

She nodded. "I went through a lot in Kansas City, but that's another story. A good friend in Chicago saved me, found a decent job for me where she worked until I started making money with my camera." She flexed her fingers on the steering wheel.

"Okay." She took a deep breath and blew it out. "I'll try to at least talk to CeCe, and if the opportunity lends itself, I'll talk to her father as well. I'm not promising anything. Like I said, this isn't my deal. I'd like to enjoy the rest of my stay here."

"Fair enough. Turn on the other side of the dam. We'll get to Will's just as the sun comes up."

"Un-uh, I'm taking you home first."

"No way! I'll call my grandma from Will's, so she won't be worried. I'm sticking to you like glue, so you won't back out on talking to CeCe."

"How am I going to explain to Marney that I was out all night with you?"

Doug grinned. "Tell her you like younger men."

Chapter 13

The loud strains of "Courageous," by Casting Crowns, roused Clay Woods from a deep fog of sleep. He lay sprawled across a log cabin quilt in his uniform. Eyes closed, he reached for the cell phone.

"Yeah." He raked hair back from his forehead, then rubbed his eyes. The soft, but serious voice of Betty, the night dispatcher, all but whispered in his ear.

"What? Sorry Betty. I can barely hear you. Who're you talking about? Larkin who?" He sat on the side of the bed, cradled the phone between his shoulder and chin, leaned over and slipped on his shoes.

"Oh, the land developer." He made his way into the kitchen. "Betty, speak louder, please." He grabbed the coffeepot and walked to the sink.

"When did that happen? Okay, I'll be right there. I'll check in with Marney over at Will Darnell's place first. Yeah, her city friend is missing. We think she got lost in the woods and couldn't find her way out before dark." He glanced out the window.

"I need to get a search party together to go look for her, but I've got to check out the shooting, too. Please call some guys on the list of search volunteers and have them go over to Will's. Marney can fill them in."

Clay looked at the coffeepot, then set it back on the stove. "Yeah, the excitement always happens after you go home." He glanced at his watch.

"Okay, I'm going to grab a cup of coffee at the convenience store, then I'll go over there. Tell that Biggs guy to stay put."

He set the phone on the kitchen table, turned on the faucet and splashed handfuls of cold water over his face, then grabbed a terry dish towel from a drawer and dried.

Jeb's number rang ten times.

Out like a light. I'll probably have a hard time getting him awake when I get over there.

A few miles down the road, Clay made a call from his patrol car. "Marney? Clay here. Any sign of Will and Otis, or Rally?" He punched the speaker button and placed the phone on a dashboard dock.

"Will and Otis made it home. They're both okay, but tired. I think they had a little adventure."

"Well, that's a relief. At least they're home. I'll make a run over to the Crest View Motel. That land developer Biggs stays over there. Seems there was a problem in his cabin a while ago. I'll go check it out, then I'll be right over. Jeb doesn't answer his phone, so it might take me a bit to rouse him. I'd rather have him with me. He has a habit of taking off on his own to investigate things. I don't need him adding his own form of chaos."

He eased to a stop at a red light, pulled forward when it changed to green. "Put on a pot of coffee, would you? I didn't take time to make any. I'll see you when I'm finished at the Crest View." He leaned forward and ended the call.

Chapter 14

R ally saw two heads silhouetted against the window as she pulled into the parking area in front of the house. She punched Doug in the shoulder to wake him.

"Looks like we have a welcoming committee. I would bet they've been up all night."

"Ah, gee whiz. I hate that." Doug stretched. "They're gonna be plenty mad at me."

Will opened the door and waited for them to get out of the car. Rally watched him turn to Marney, his voice loud enough to hear as they approached. "Why does she have that Doug kid with her?"

"Who knows?" Marney answered. "I'm relieved she's safe, but I'm also aggravated. She's caused some problems. I'm not going easy on her."

Rally and Doug pushed through the door at the same time and headed for the sofa in the living room. The smell of coffee and fresh baked biscuits hit them in the face.

"Don't ask." Rally sprawled across half of the sofa. "Something smells wonderful."

"That's for the search party that will be here any minute to get out and comb the woods for you," Marney said. She watched Doug plop down on the other end of the couch and stretch his long legs out on the large hassock in front of him.

Marney stood with her hands on her hips, looking down at Rally. "And I *will* ask. Where have you been? And what are you doing with Doug?"

"Please give me a few minutes to rest. It's been a long night. I'm okay. Doug's okay. That's all that matters right now."

"Well, good for you, but we're not okay. Will and Otis went out into those woods last night looking for you. Otis took off after some raccoon and Will like to never found him. They were out there all night."

The hound sprawled on a braided rug in front of the warm oven. He raised his head when he heard his name, but dropped it back down and closed his eyes.

Will went into the kitchen, poured coffee into two mugs, and took them into the living room. "Yeah, but the good news is, Otis still has his smeller."

Rally pulled an afghan from the back of the sofa and draped it over her body. "I'm happy for Otis. Now, may we please rest a bit? I promise we'll tell you everything as soon as we drink our coffee and wake up a little."

"Well, you won't get to rest long," Will said. "Clay is on his way over here to organize a search party as soon as he takes care of another call. He's sure got a surprise coming."

"I wasn't lost. I was at the lake." Rally looked at Doug.

"All this time? Clay said he talked to you there, but you left. He said you called in about a sinking truck."

"My truck." Doug shifted his weight and slid down to rest his head on the arm of the sofa.

Will set a coffee mug on the table next to Doug. He bent

down and boomed into his ear. "What was your truck doing in the lake?"

Doug bolted upright. "Dang, old man. Did you have to yell? Just because you're deaf doesn't mean everybody is. I don't know why my truck was in the lake. I think somebody knocked me on the head. All I know is, I got out of it before I drowned."

Marney sat down on the edge of a kitchen chair and stared at the two people on the sofa as though they were strangers. "You nearly drowned? I'm not believing any of this."

"That was before I kidnapped Rally and took her hostage ... but I didn't harm her. See, she's okay."

"Get out of here." Marney stared at them. "This is the craziest thing I've ever heard. What did you want with her?"

"I didn't want her. I was hiding in her car until the fuss was over, then I was going to take it 'cause mine was in the lake. But she wouldn't shut up and let me steal it, so I had to take her hostage and make her drive me to safety."

"Yeah, your safety. Not mine." Rally sat up and took the cup of coffee Will offered her. She shook her head. "Okay, you won't leave us alone until we tell you the entire story. There isn't much more than what you already know. We stayed in a cabin back in the boonies until Doug finally decided it was safe to leave."

He grinned and poked her in the arm. "You decided I wasn't scary anymore. That's why we left."

Rally scowled. "You weren't scary to begin with. I suppose I'll have to go over this again when that deputy sheriff gets here. What's his name again?"

"Clay Woods. You know his name," Marney said. "And yes, he will want to ask questions. You've caused some problems and sounds like Doug has, too. Clay is on a call at the Crest View Motel. Biggs, the guy that's in town wanting to build a housing development, had the owner call about a disturbance at his cabin. This has been one busy night for Clay."

Rally and Doug turned and stared at each other. Doug sat straight up and looked at Marney. "Biggs? Larkin Biggs? What's up with him?"

"I don't know. Clay didn't say. There was a disturbance."

"The Monarch Moon," Doug nodded. "I noticed it on the way to the cabin. It's a full moon. You know what they say about a full moon during the Monarch migration?"

Marney threw her hands into the air. "That's a bunch of hogwash. That has nothing to do with anything."

"Oh yes, it does," Will chimed into the conversation. "Weird things happen during the Monarch Moon. My mama used to tell stories about strange things goin' on. Why, I could tell you tales—"

"Not now, Will." Marney pointed a finger at the two seated on the sofa. "We don't have time for that. We need to hear the rest of their story."

Doug averted his eyes away from her. "Will's right. We always got more calls when there was a full moon during the migration. Anyone who ever worked in an emergency room can tell you that. They're busier during a full moon, but during a Monarch Moon, those nights are crazier."

Rally rubbed her forehead. "This place is strange, period. I don't know how a bunch of butterflies flying over could make it stranger but, right now, nothing makes more sense to me than that."

Chapter 15

The Crest View Motel sat in the woods five miles east of the Monarch Moon city limits. It did not offer luxurious accommodation but, hidden away from tourist traffic and far enough out, it felt like the country. Clay's old classmate, Brett Hawkins, kept the place clean and well maintained. His wife, the former Geneva Burk, a pretty girl Clay had gone out with a few times his senior year, planted flowers every spring around the entrance, cabins, pool, and outbuildings. Everyone in the community envied her ability to keep flowers blooming through the hottest, driest summers.

Clay pulled the cruiser under the striped charcoal-gray-and-white canopy. Everything about the Crest View was tasteful. Geneva had a way with flea market and estate sale finds. He knew little about decorating, but he always admired how nice the place looked.

Brett walked out of the entrance and waited for him. He was chewing on a toothpick.

"Howdy, Deputy." He tapped the bill of his Crest View cap with two fingers, a typical Ozarks country greeting.

"Morning, Brett. What's going on?" He got out and walked around the cruiser.

"Well..." The owner scratched his head, pointed over Clay's right shoulder. "The guy over in cabin ten says somebody shot at him." He nodded toward the row closest to the woods. "He threw all kinds of fits, then took off. I don't know if he was scared or mad, maybe both. I told him I called the law, but he took off anyway. Said he wasn't spending another night here until I got some security."

Clay turned and looked behind him. "You were over there?"

"Heck no. I was waiting for protection to get here. No sense me getting shot at, too." He grinned, moved the toothpick over to the other side of his mouth with his tongue.

"You thinking he imagined it?" Clay pulled sunglasses out of his shirt pocket and stepped from under the canopy into the sunlight.

"I heard a shot. Could have been a hunter got a little close and popped one off, might've sounded like it was right outside his window. Biggs says it broke and shattered the glass, though. I would guess it to be a stray shot." He leaned against the hood of the cruiser. "He ain't hurt."

"All right then." Clay walked to the car and opened the door. "I'll need you to bring a key. I'm sure he locked up before he left."

Brett pulled a key out of his pocket. "Figured you'd say that." He opened the passenger door, ducked his head, and settled into the seat. He looked at Clay, a mischievous grin spread across his face. "Hit the siren? One short one?"

The friends Clay grew up with seemed to think they had an inside track on getting him to do things with his authority they could not. Turn on the siren, hit the lights, run a red light, do all three at the same time. It didn't matter how many times he said "no," they kept trying.

"Better not. This isn't an emergency and there's nobody in my way. You know that."

Brett shrugged. "It's always worth a try, friend."

"You and Jeb are gonna drive me nuts. You both need to grow up. Chasing sirens is for kids, which we are not anymore."

"You're the only one who grew up, Deputy. Too bad, too. You were a lot more fun before you took to the law and religion." He slapped his leg and laughed. "You and your cousin are no more alike than moonshine and soda pop. If it hadn't been for you, he more than likely would've grown up in juvie."

Clay steered the cruiser into the parking space in front of the cabin. He sat for a moment, then turned to look at his friend.

"We all do what we think is right for us. I choose to serve. You choose to provide lodging for people who need a place to stay. In Jeb's case, he does what he's always done. Float along on the edge. Live off the goodwill and kindness of others. I promised Aunt Lizzie I would look after him, but I refused to make his life easy." He unfastened the seatbelt and opened his door.

"I will be there for him, like I will for you and the rest of my friends. That doesn't mean you get to run the siren and lights or play cops and robbers in my car." He grinned, punched his friend in the arm.

"Now, let's look at this cabin before I chase down its occupant and get his statement."

Chapter 16

Will shuffled into the living room from the kitchen with a fresh pot of coffee.

"Well, it's so. The migration during a full moon creates havoc. Ask the deputy when he gets here. He's always busier when it happens."

"And how often does 'it' happen?" Rally asked.

Doug's expression grew thoughtful for a moment. "Oh, I don't know. It's hard to say. Mother Nature gets to movin' things around and sometimes she sends those butterflies at the same time there's a full moon and—"

Rally stuck a hand, palm out, toward Doug's face. "Stop right there. That's the most absurd thing I've ever heard. I won't sit here and listen to you blame those gorgeous little butterflies for mysterious things happening. That's just crazy. This place doesn't need a full moon, or butterflies, or anything else to make it curious."

Marney laughed. "Wait a minute, young lady. Don't be calling our town 'curious.' We're quite ordinary, compared to what I've seen in the city."

"Well, yeah. But there's a lot more people in the city. I'll admit, though, it gets crazy sometimes." She stuck her palm out toward Marney. "Touche."

Marney slapped Rally's hand for a high-five.

"There are *unusual* people everywhere." Will pointed at Doug. "You take some of his family. His Uncle Luther was a piece of work."

"Don't talk about my family being strange, Will Darnell. I don't recall any of them taking off in the dead of night with an old hound dog that needed to be put out of his misery years ago. You're both way too old to be wandering around through those woods, full moon or not."

Will stood over Doug, his fists clenched. "Why, you smart aleck young pup. I ought to—"

"That's enough." Marney moved between the two men. "Bantering back and forth serves no purpose. It's obvious none of us have had enough sleep. Everyone's nerves are on edge. We'll wait for Clay to get here, then we'll all get some rest after he leaves." She nodded toward the younger man.

"Doug, nobody's going to feel like driving you over to your grandmother's house until later. I would ask Clay to take you, but I think he's got his hands full."

"Thanks, Marney, but I expect Clay will want to give me some free lodging down at the jail." Doug gave Rally a sideways glance. "After all, I am a kidnapper."

Rally patted his arm. "Oh, don't worry, Doug. I won't press charges. I'll tell the deputy we were ... well, I don't know what I'll tell him, but I'll think of something."

Doug shook his head. "To tell you the truth, I can't think of any good reason for us to have been there together except for you to have gone against your will."

"I'll tell him you were showing me the cabin because I was interested in renting it next summer, and my car stalled. We couldn't get it started." Rally hesitated for a moment.

"Do you know who owns that cabin?"

Doug frowned in thought. "I think it's for sale. Joe and Mary Marsh owned it until Mary passed away a year after Joe. They left it to their son. He never comes down here. I heard the other day, Lakeside Realty has it listed for sale. My friend Bill Jacobs said they hired him to come clean up the area and resurface the lane. He asked if I'd like to help him, said he'd split fifty-fifty with me."

"There you go." Rally bumped his arm with her fist. "You're practically a part of the sales team. You had a legitimate right to show me the cabin. I mentioned I was looking for a place here and you knew of one."

"That all sounds fine, but since the deputy thinks I may have drowned, and I'm going to tell him someone tried to murder me, how are you going to explain how you were in my company?"

"Don't worry. I'll think of something after I've had more coffee and some rest. My mind is numb right now. I'll come up with a story. Go along with me, Doug, whatever I say. It's that or maybe go to jail."

Will raised an eyebrow. "You'd best tell the truth. Nothin' good ever comes from telling lies. Clay's a fair man. He'll listen and do the right thing. The joker that pushed Doug's truck into the lake needs to be found." His attention shifted to the window. "Here comes the deputy now, and he's got Jeb with him."

"Oh, no." Marney slapped her hand against her forehead. "Not him again."

"What about him?" Rally asked.

"It seems Jeb is mighty fond of Marney's coffee." Will looked at his niece. "At least that's what she said when Otis and I got home from the woods. I went to get a cup, and the pot was bone dry. She said Jeb drank it all while he looked at her all moon eyed."

"Do you have to tell everything you hear? That was

private, and I only told you because I was so disgusted." She stared at her uncle, arms crossed over her chest. "I can't tell you anything."

Rally sat up straight and bunched the afghan around her shoulders. "Ooh. Marney has a new beau. Be sure and introduce me."

"Don't be funny. Wait until you see him. He's the most obnoxious guy in the whole county. I think we told you he's Clay's cousin. They grew up together. I don't know how Clay puts up with him."

"Jeb loves that patrol cruiser," Doug said. "He hitches a ride with Clay every chance he gets. I'd be willing to bet if Clay ever left the keys in it and Jeb got half a chance, he'd take it for another joy ride."

"Better hush up. They're getting ready to come in." Will shuffled over to the door. "Come on in, Deputy. Hey there, Jeb."

"How's it goin' Will?" Jeb followed Clay through the open door.

"Little tired, and a lot sleepy. Yourself?" He closed the door and motioned for the two men to find a seat.

"I'm good. Got a few winks before Clay come after me." Jeb looked past Will and grinned. "Got any coffee there, Miss Marney?"

"I had some ready for Clay, then these two came in and depleted the pot." She kept her focus away from him.

Jeb leaned against the door frame. "Suppose you could make another one?"

"I'll make another pot, but only because of Clay." Marney scowled. "I sure wouldn't go to any trouble for you. You are way too presumptuous."

Rally nudged Doug, nodded toward Jeb, who was following Marney into the kitchen. Doug covered his mouth with a sofa pillow. His squinted eyes gave away the grin he was trying to hide.

"That wouldn't be buttermilk biscuits I smell, would it?"

Jeb sniffed the air. "I didn't get to eat before the deputy here picked me up."

"Well, you should have asked him to stop at the convenience store for coffee and a couple of donuts. This is not a short-order cafe. I'll fix breakfast for my family and friends when I get around to it." Marney turned to look at the deputy. "That includes you Clay, if you'd like to stay."

"You're welcome to eat with us, too, Jeb." Will gave his niece a stern look.

Jeb slid into a kitchen chair, but Clay motioned him to a chair by the door.

"Thanks, Marney, but I'm up to my ears in work. I'll grab something later. I need a few minutes, though, to talk to your two guests." He walked to the sofa where Doug and Rally sat. He nodded at Doug.

"I'm curious where you've been. We pulled your truck out of the lake early yesterday afternoon. Would you like to explain how it got there?"

Rally watched Deputy Wood's body language as Doug related the previous day's events. He frowned, looked Doug in the eye. She wondered what was going through his mind as he made notes on the clipboard. She hoped he believed Doug.

Finished with Doug, he turned his attention to her. For a moment, their eyes met, and Rally felt herself respond to his gaze. Something about this tall, quiet man appealed to her, although she fought the emotion.

"Do you want to press charges against Doug, Miss Chandler?"

"No. He didn't mean any harm. I think he was desperate, not knowing who was after him or what he should do. Who would have used better judgment under those circumstances? Besides, I believe his story. Sounds to me like this Larkin Biggs is out to get whatever he can in whatever way it takes."

The deputy shook his head. "I'm not so sure he's behind

this. He says someone was taking potshots at him last night. I was at the Crest View, investigating his call before I came over here."

Marney filled the enamel carafe from the coffeepot and then went through the process of making another pot. Jeb jumped up from his chair and hurried over to help.

"Let me take that for you, Miss Marney. I'll fill everyone's mugs." He put an arm around her shoulder and reached for the carafe with the other hand.

The unexpected reaction of Marney shrugging his arm away just as he picked up the carafe caused him to lose his grip. She grabbed at the toppling container at the same time he tried to recover it. She righted it, but Jeb grabbed her arm and pulled her to him.

"Get your hands off me." She shivered. "Ooh, get away. Don't touch me!" She grabbed a spatula and swatted his hand.

All three of the men in the living area started toward the kitchen, but Clay moved in front of Will and Doug. "Jeb. That's enough."

"Hey, I was trying to help. If she hadn't jerked when she did, it would have been okay."

Marney stooped to wipe up spilled coffee, then stood and pointed at the floor.

"Mud, Jeb. You've tracked it everywhere. Get those shoes off and take them outside."

Jeb lowered his shoulders, looked down at the floor like a kid caught eating out of the sugar bowl. "Okay, okay. Don't get bent out of shape. I'll get 'em off."

A muddy trail of footprints stood out like fried chicken at a vegan picnic. They ran across the floor to the kitchen sink and back. He tiptoed toward the door, but the damage was done. She'd given him no recourse but to slink away.

"Where'd you find mud around here this morning?" Will looked down at Jeb's feet. "It ain't rained enough to create mud in over a week."

"Ah, I guess I got it at the lake." Jeb swallowed and looked at the four people staring at him. "When I was out there, helpin' pull Doug's truck out."

"That was yesterday," Clay said. "Any mud from the lake would be dry by now. This is fresh. You must have picked it up this morning." He walked over to Jeb and motioned for him to sit back down in the designated chair. "I'm headed for the car, anyway. I'll carry them out for you. No reason for both of us going."

"Yeah, well, I watered some bushes when I got home. They looked like they were dying. Must have stepped in the water that fell off them, then walked across the dirt in the driveway. That's probably what happened."

He sat down, pulled his shoes off and handed them to Clay. "Take care of them, cuz. Them's my best running shoes, you know." He looked down at the floor to avoid eye contact.

"Don't worry." Clay opened the door and took the shoes outside.

Marney walked to the utility closet and pulled out a mop and a bucket. "I just mopped that floor and I'm not cleaning up after you."

Jeb crossed his arms over his chest and straightened himself tall in the chair. "I don't do woman's work."

All eyes focused on Marney.

"You will mop up those tracks, or I'm gonna tell your cousin you stole that whiskey from the liquor store. Will saw you carrying it out the day he went up to meet Rally."

"You can't prove nothin'." Jeb remained in his chair and stared straight ahead.

"Will called the store. Mr. Cross said it's not the first time he's noticed liquor disappearing after you've been in there. I'm sick of you getting away with things because people hate to call Clay and tell him."

Jeb tried to stare Marney down, but she stood over him, a bucket in one hand, the mop in the other. He finally got up, ambled over to the sink, and filled the bucket with water.

"Don't forget to rinse with clear water when you're finished and make sure all the mud is gone." She squirted some all-purpose cleanser in the bucket and pointed at the marks.

Clay walked back into the house. "Miss Chandler, would you mind coming out to the patrol car with me for a moment? I have a few more questions. My clipboard's in the cruiser. I forgot to bring it in." He looked not at her face, but into her eyes. She sensed more to his request than what he expressed.

"It's Rally. Sure. Give me a minute." She reached down and pulled her boots on, wrapped the afghan around her shoulders, and followed the deputy outside.

"What is it? What couldn't you ask me in there? You don't doubt Doug's story, do you? He's telling the truth. He is *so* concerned about CeCe. I know he's telling the truth."

"Please. Calm down." Clay opened the cruiser's passenger door for Rally. "I'm going to leave in a few minutes, and I'm making sure Jeb goes with me. My concern is Doug staying here. I'm not sure he's out of danger, and I don't want him here putting the rest of you in harm's way."

"What do you mean? How could we be in danger, and what does that have to do with Jeb?"

"When I went out to investigate Biggs' complaint at the motel, there was wet ground under the window of his cabin. I tracked down the water source. An outside faucet was leaking all the way down that side of the cabin. I found some footprints in the mud. I'm going to check them against the imprints I made of Jeb's shoes when I brought them outside. There was some time between the incident at the Crest View and when I picked Jeb up, but I got good prints of both. I also found a fired shotgun shell close to Biggs' window."

"Why would Jeb be shooting at that land developer, and what does that have to do with Doug?"

"I don't know, but I'm going to find out. Another thing that concerns me is Jeb's four-wheeler parked in his driveway. He always keeps it in an outbuilding behind his trailer. The hood was warm when I touched it. Since we left his truck here, it was his only transportation. He could easily have ridden it through the woods to Crest View."

Clay shifted in his seat and looked toward the house. "I wonder if I could ask you to make sure Doug goes somewhere safe. That cabin is off limits. Jeb heard him talk about it. Even though he didn't say exactly how to get there, Jeb's familiar enough with this area to know any abandoned cabins. Maybe you could ask CeCe if she knows a place he can go?"

"Me? She doesn't know me. We had one brief conversation. Why would she even talk to me about Doug? I think she's trying to stay away from him. Can't you lock Jeb up, so he won't be a threat?"

"I could, but I don't have enough evidence yet, and I don't think he's working alone. He has no reason to be after Doug. Someone is putting him up to it. He doesn't have a reason to be after the developer either. Besides, he isn't smart enough to plan this stuff on his own. Another strange thing, he hasn't been working for several weeks, but he suddenly has money enough to buy some new gear and go out diving almost every day. He doesn't own a boat, so he must be helping buy gas for someone else's."

"Maybe the diving buddy is involved." She shivered, pulled the afghan closer. "Do you mind?" She pointed at the heater.

He started the car. "Sorry. It should warm up in a few minutes." He reached into the back seat, pulled his service jacket over, wrapped it around her shoulders, and tucked it under her chin.

"Bill Harris has a family and works a steady evening job

for decent pay. He wouldn't hang out with Jeb if he wasn't such an excellent diver. No, if he has an accomplice, it's somebody who has a reason to want Doug and the developer out of the way. I think it's somebody with money, and they're hiring Jeb to do their dirty work."

"Do you usually share your suspicions with strangers, Deputy?"

"I don't have a choice on this one. You're smart, and I think you're gutsy. Keep an eye out and let me know if Jeb turns up around here again. I'm taking him with me, but I can't guarantee his whereabouts all the time. Meanwhile, see if you can talk Doug into hiding out a while longer." He handed her a business card. "Here's my cell number. Call me if you need me."

She looked at the card, tucked it into her jeans pocket. She thought about the possibility of Fenner figuring out that she was spending time with Marney. He was smart. He knew people in Texas who knew her background, where she grew up and who her friends were.

If I were in trouble, would Deputy Clay Woods come to my rescue?

They went inside. Jeb, finished with his "woman's work," engaged in small talk with Will and Doug. Marney wrapped warm biscuits in a tea towel and handed the bundle to Clay, along with a thermal coffee cup to go. He said his goodbyes and cautioned everyone to get some sleep and let him know if they heard about any unusual activities in the area, then motioned for Jeb to go out the door ahead of him.

Will handed Jeb a travel cup of coffee and two biscuits on a cloth napkin.

"Enjoy them, son."

Jeb nodded. "Much obliged, Will."

~ ~ ~ ~

"How did I get involved in this whole mess?" Rally muttered under her breath as she stared out the window and watched the cruiser turn onto the gravel road. "Now I'm playing detective, watch-dogging this house and a guy that took me hostage last night. How did this happen?"

"What are you mumbling about over there?"

Rally turned away from the window. "Nothing, just fussing to myself."

Will put his coffee cup in the sink. "I'm going up and catch a few winks before I go out and do my chores. Things can wait that long. Y'all better get some rest, too." He headed toward the stairs.

"That sounds good to me." Doug stood in the middle of the living room and stretched. "If you'll point me in the right direction, Marney—"

Rally turned and looked at Doug. "Oh no. I need you to go with me. Remember, you wanted me to talk to CeCe?"

He dropped both arms to his sides and stared at her. "Well, yeah, but don't we need to rest first?"

"I think I'm okay." She looked at her watch. "What time do they open?"

"Early, about 7:00 a.m. so people can run by before work."

"I'll get a quick shower, then we can go. We'd better take care of it as soon as possible. You never know what that slimeball might talk her into doing. You don't have to go into the pharmacy with me, but I would like you to be in the car for moral support. She might tell me to mind my own business. I might have to get her to come out to the car, so we can both talk to her."

"She won't talk to me, but if it'll make you feel better, I'll go along. I'll wash up a little and try to make myself more presentable. I don't want her dad to see me out in the car. He would run me off for sure. You'd better park down the street from the pharmacy."

"Good idea. I'll freshen up as soon as I've helped

Marney."

"You go on." Marney waved her off toward the hall bathroom. "It's only a few coffee mugs." She opened the door to a linen closet and handed Doug a big, fluffy towel.

"You can wash up in the kitchen. I'm going upstairs to lie down for a few minutes myself. I'll set my alarm, so I don't oversleep. Besides biscuits, there're some cinnamon rolls in the pie safe. You may help yourselves to as many as you want. That might hold you until we get a decent meal down you. I'll have lunch ready at noon. Make sure the two of you get back by then."

"Thanks, Marney." Doug's eyes focused on the tin safe with the shape of a star punched in the front. "I *am* getting hungry. That coffee was great, but it's not doing much for my growling stomach."

He patted Marney's shoulder. "You've been great. I really appreciate it."

"No problem, Doug." Marney smiled.

The thought of a homemade cinnamon roll made Rally want to forget about the shower.

"Doug. Save a couple for me. I get mean when I'm hungry."

Chapter 17

The coffee worked for Rally, but she had serious doubts about Doug. Sleep seemed to be his number one priority. Clay's urgency in finding a hiding place for her charge stimulated her as much as the caffeine. She glanced at her napping passenger.

"You need to hide."

His head rolled to one side and rested on his shoulder.

"Huh … what? What did you say?" He rubbed his eyes.

"I said you must hide out somewhere. Not back at the cabin, either."

"What are you talking about?" He straightened up in the seat and combed sandy blond hair away from his face with his fingers.

"Clay believes you're still in danger. Whoever put your truck in the lake might try to harm you again. He thinks CeCe would know of somewhere safe."

Doug yawned and stretched. "Makes sense. Who knows out-of-the-way places around here better than CeCe?"

"Wouldn't you know the same ones?"

"Nah. In the past, she and her girlfriends would meet up in remote locations in the countryside, to make sure boys wouldn't intrude on their gatherings."

"Why so secretive?"

"You should be able to answer that. You were that age once. Didn't you and Marney ever do any secret girl stuff?"

Rally thought back to her teenage years. Images blossomed.

"Come to think of it, we did. We sat in the fork of an old mulberry tree and looked at department store sale brochures. We picked out clothes and shoes. Marney drooled over pots and pans, cooking utensils, that kind of thing. Her dream was to be a master chef."

"What was *your* dream?"

"The cameras, all the photography stuff. I wanted to be a famous photographer." She frowned. "The closest Marney got was cooking for her family after her mother died. She was always feeding people. I think that's why she had so many boyfriends in high school. She invited them for dinner."

"What about you?"

"I saved my babysitting money to get my first camera, a used 35mm Pentax. I took pictures for the high school yearbooks, portraits of relatives and friends. It wasn't until my senior year I realized that photography could be art. Books at the library taught me framing, composition, the rule of thirds, the basics. Then I bought a nice digital, won a few contests, and there was no turning back. I was hooked."

"Was Marney a chef in a fancy restaurant?"

"No. She went to college and worked part-time as a secretary for an attorney. She liked it so much she ended up majoring in pre-law."

"Marney, a lawyer? Wow."

"Yeah, I know. When her aunt died, she gave up law

school, and a guy she cared about, to come and look after Will. He had health issues, and she was his only kin left."

"Darn. That's tough. Will said she needed help, and he took her in."

"No." Rally shook her head. "She said she had to let Will think he was taking care of her."

"Hey, don't worry. I won't say a word. I like Will and Marney both. They have a good thing goin'. I wouldn't want to mess it up for them. Will *is* stubborn. Marney's smart, handling things the way she does."

Rally glanced from the road to Doug. "Speaking of taking care of people, did you call your grandmother?"

"Hmm? Oh, yeah, about Grandma. I need to talk to you." He twisted in the seat to face her. "She's not happy about me hiding out, and I'm not happy about her being there alone. What if Larkin Biggs comes back while I'm gone and tries to bully her into selling our property? Without me there, she might cave."

"So, how do we prevent that?"

He turned to look through the side window. "You need to go get her."

She gripped the wheel. "What did you say? Speak up. I can't hear what you're muttering about over there."

He faced her again. "Please, go get her and take her to Will's."

She raised an eyebrow. "Why should I do that?"

"Because." He took a deep breath. "She's a defenseless little old lady who needs protection, even though she doesn't think so. I doubt it will be easy to get her to go." His voice lowered. "Stay between her and the shotgun that's propped inside the door on the right."

Chapter 18

Rally parked Blue in the alley behind the pharmacy and turned off the engine.

"Hunker down. Stay out of sight. We don't want CeCe's dad to see you."

Doug grumbled but scrunched down in the seat.

The soft peal of a bell announced her arrival as she entered the store through the rear entrance. She made her way down the hallway, past the bathrooms, the office, and a storage area. On the right was a room with a thick door she assumed was where the drugs were. Its accessibility to the alley seemed too easy, in her opinion, but then she remembered she was in a small town with a low crime rate, not like the city where she lived.

As she approached the center aisle, she heard someone talking near the soda fountain. CeCe stood behind the counter with a cell phone against her ear.

"Who would do that?" she spoke in a hushed voice. "Where were you, inside or out?"

Rally moved closer to the conversation and perused the wide assortment of pain relievers, trying to listen without appearing to be eavesdropping,

"Doug would not do that out of jealousy. He knows I want a career. It's dove season. Maybe a hunter misjudged his shot. I'm sure there's a logical explanation."

CeCe glanced into a mirror over the doorway.

"I've got to go. I have a customer. See you tonight? Okay. I'll tell Dad I'm going to the movies with Sarah. Later." She hurried down the aisle toward Rally.

"You're out bright and early this morning. Can I help you with something?"

"It was a sleepless night, and yes, I hope you can help me. I need to ask a big favor."

"Okay, sure." CeCe waved a hand over the analgesics. "Most of these medications are your standard stuff. The directions and side effects are on the label. What's the problem? Headache, backache?"

"No, my pain has a specific name. It's Doug."

"Doug? What about Doug? I heard they found his truck in the lake. I suppose he lost control and couldn't get it stopped. He's been reckless. He got upset with me when he was in here yesterday." She shrugged. "You were here. We've had some disagreements lately. My dad blames him for me not going back to school."

"Yeah," Rally said. "I heard all about that from Doug, but he thinks it's that land shark who's trying to sell you some yarn about modeling school."

CeCe stepped back, drew in a breath. "A yarn? It's no yarn. He's got me set to start after Christmas. It's my dream to be a model. Doug doesn't want me to leave school either. I'm grateful that he cares, but I need to do what I think is best for me."

"Look girl," Rally settled her weight on one hip. "I'd love to tell you all the reasons you shouldn't believe this guy, but I don't have time right now. The evening was exhausting, and I've got a sleepy puppy in my car who needs a place to hide."

She touched CeCe's shoulder. "I've heard the same promises, but from a different angle. They were lies. I'll explain later. Just promise me you won't leave with this guy until I talk to you again, okay?"

CeCe nodded. "I don't have plans to go anywhere soon."

"We'll talk later. I need you to help me figure out a place for Doug to disappear to for a few days, and I ask that you not share this with anyone. Deputy Woods suggested I come to you for help."

"Why does Doug need to hide?"

"That's another long story. What I can tell you is that Doug did not run his truck into the lake. He was in the truck, knocked out. Someone tried to kill him. Once he, or she, whoever did it, finds out he didn't drown, they may be after him again. He needs a place to hide. Will you help?"

"What?" CeCe placed a hand over her heart. "I can't believe this. Someone also shot in Larkin's cabin last evening. He thinks Doug did it. I can't imagine such a thing."

"It wasn't Doug. He was with me all night."

"With you? All night?"

Rally watched the girl's eyes widen. It could have been the green-eyed monster she detected, but more likely disbelief that Doug might have found her attractive.

She stared at her image in the soda fountain mirror. What a mess. It didn't concern her what CeCe or Doug thought, but Clay seeing her so disheveled bothered her. She straightened her shoulders, smoothed wrinkles from her shirt, and ran fingers through her windblown hair.

"Yes," she nodded. "All night. It's not what you think. We were at the cabin talking. I helped him out of a jam."

"The cabin?"

She nodded. "Doug said you two went there often."

"I hope he told you we went to the cabin to talk. My

dad didn't like him, so we had to hide."

"I know all that. Doug told me it was innocent. He said you're a good girl."

CeCe blushed. "That's sweet."

"He cares for you a lot."

"Please don't tell—"

"No worries. Where is your dad?"

"I don't know. He left a few minutes ago in a big hurry. Said for me to watch the place and have anyone with a prescription refill call back later or leave a number. He hurried off to take care of some unexpected business. I can't imagine what that might be, but he's been acting weird since we lost my mom."

"Doug told me a little about that, too. I'm sorry. I lost my dad a while back. It's tough."

"Yeah." She cast her eyes downward.

Rally watched the younger version of herself wipe a tear from her cheek.

"What about a place for Doug? Got any ideas?"

CeCe stared at the ceiling. Her face scrunched into a frown. "I'm thinking. I know a few places … but there's one where nobody would look."

"Where's that?"

"Our attic bedroom. Mom fixed it for my cousin when he worked at the amusement park over by Branson every summer. He's out of college and married now.

"My dad never goes up there. By the time he gets home after a fourteen-hour day, he eats a bite, and then falls into bed. The house might come down around him, but he won't wake up. Doug can't run in and out, though. Can't have the neighbors see him coming and going."

"I don't know him well," Rally said. "Not sure how he'd feel about that. What about you?"

"I sleep on the couch half the time. If I'm in for the evening, I fall asleep watching TV. If I go out, I raid the fridge when I get home, then crash. Doug will have to keep his distance when I'm around, but I'll make sure he's fed. He can watch TV while Dad's gone."

"It must be lonely for you with your dad working all those hours. You wouldn't see him at all if you didn't work together."

"Sometimes I think it's easier. We stay out of each other's hair that way. He works so hard, though. Before Mom died, he used to have another pharmacist work part-time so he could be home to care for her, and he always closed the pharmacy on holidays. Now, he works seven days a week. It's difficult in a small town. Everyone knows your phone number and where you live."

"I'm sorry." Rally gave the girl a quick hug.

"It's nice to know someone understands. I'm just looking forward to getting out of here and into modeling school. Things will be better."

"Don't count on that. We'll talk later. I've got to get back to Doug. Thanks, CeCe. And whatever you do, keep Doug's presence at your house a secret. Most of all, don't tell Larson Biggs."

"I wouldn't dare tell him. He doesn't like Doug, says he's trouble. You'll let me know what's going on, won't you?"

"I'm sure things will be okay in a day or two. Deputy Woods wants to have time to investigate leads before he feels it's safe for Doug to be seen anywhere. And CeCe, even though your friend Mr. Biggs had that encounter at the motel, please share nothing I've told you. The less said, the better."

"I understand. Meet me in the alley behind our house after dark. Tell Doug to be quiet. The neighbor has a dog."

Chapter 19

With Doug handed over to CeCe, Rally followed his directions to the mobile home park and his grandmother, Eunice Hargrove. From the sound of Doug's end of the phone conversation, Eunice was reluctant to budge from her home. Who knew what might happen when she arrived to take her to Will's?

She lowered her speed as she steered into the vacation traffic creeping across the dam. Tourists gawked at the diamond-like sparkles of moonlight reflecting off shimmering waves on Paradise Lake. She would love to be standing at the top of one of the mountainous side roads, capturing it all with a camera.

A few miles on the other side of the bridge, she saw the sign that announced the entry to the Easy Living Mobile Home Park. She took the first left and pulled up in front of the building marked Office.

"Mrs. Hargrove?" Rally rapped on the door. "Mrs. Hargrove, your grandson Doug sent me. Please open the door. I'm a friend."

A soft voice answered. "What is it you want?"

"I'm Rally Chandler. Doug talked to you, told you I was coming? It might not be safe for you to stay here."

"It's that developer, ain't it?" The voice grew stronger. "He was out here again yesterday. He's no good. I can tell by looking into his beady eyes. Where's Doug?"

"Doug is fine. He's away for a few days. That's why I'm here. He trusts me to watch after you. He told you that. But to do it, I need to take you with me."

The door opened. A tiny woman with a gray bun knotted on the back of her head stepped aside and allowed Rally to enter.

A small desk with a swivel chair sat across from the door. A macramé hanger dangled from the ceiling in front of the window. Spider plants cascaded from a pot cradled in the center.

"I'm not much for staying away from home. I've got Henry's old shotgun. That and this trailer park are the only things he left me, but at least I can halfway make a living and defend myself. I suppose I should be thankful for that. He didn't leave me with a bunch of bills to pay, like Lois Willford's husband." She cocked her gray head to one side and looked up at Rally. "Were you acquainted with Harold Willford?"

"No, I wasn't. I'm new to town. I don't know anyone. Just Marney and Will ... and Doug, of course."

Eunice put a thin finger to her lips. "Ah, yes. The new blonde everyone's been talking about, although I think they've exaggerated some ... not what I expected." Eunice looked her up and down. "Too skinny."

"I'm sorry if I don't meet your expectations, but we need to get moving. I have a lot to take care of. Do you have a suitcase? You may be gone a couple of days."

"Suitcase? Why do I need a suitcase? Doug said nothing about stayin' overnight. He said he wanted me to go visit, not move in."

"Eunice, may I call you Eunice?"

"Miss Eunice, please. That's what everyone calls me."

"Miss Eunice, you need to understand. Whoever is looking for Doug could try to cause trouble for you. No telling what they might do. That's why Doug wants you to be with Marney and her uncle. It's only a couple of days, then you can come back home."

"Me, stay in the same house with Will Darnell? I don't like the idea of hangin' around that old reprobate." She folded her arms across her chest.

"Doug wouldn't ask you to leave if he didn't think it was necessary." Rally reached out and touched her shoulder. "Please, you need to trust him."

"Hmm." She uncrossed her arms. "I'll humor him on this one, but I won't make a habit of up and leaving whenever. If he's concerned about my safety here, then I'm concerned about his. I wish you would tell me where he is and what's going on."

"Doug will tell you soon enough. Let's get a few things packed. We need to get out of here."

"Okay. I'll do it, but I'm only taking a nightgown and a dress for church tomorrow. That's all I'll need. You going to church in the morning?"

"Church? No."

"Don't you attend Sunday service?"

"I used to, but it's been a long time ago. Besides, I've been up all night. I need to get some rest."

"Well, I think the good Lord would be pleased if you slept tonight and went to church in the morning."

~ ~ ~ ~

Thirty minutes later, Rally pulled to a stop in front of Will's house. Marney walked to the car to meet them.

"Welcome, Miss Eunice. Doug called to let us know you were coming. We're happy to have you stay with us. I'm sure you'll be back home soon, after Doug gets this mess ironed out."

"What I want to know is what mess you're talkin' about. All I've heard is that someone is after Doug, and that he thinks it's not safe for me to stay in the park by myself. That's a bunch of hogwash. I can take care of yours truly."

Rally gave Marney a look over Eunice's head. "We haven't discussed many of the details yet. It's taken time to get things moving in this direction."

"Oh." Marney nodded. "I see. Well, I'm sure it's nothing bad, Miss Eunice. I think Doug's concerned that the guy who wants to buy you out might get a little pushy. That's all. He doesn't want you to deal with him alone."

"I can deal with that buzzard. He needs a swift kick where the sun don't shine, or some buckshot unloaded in that area. I've never met anyone so hardheaded and obnoxious in my life."

Will opened the screen door and made his way down the path to the car. "Well, if it ain't the Widder Hargrove, come to visit a spell. Where's your grip, young lady?"

"Don't get all cutesy with me, Will Darnell. I'd just as soon smack you a good one as look at you. I know your kind."

"Now, is that any way to talk to an old friend and a prospective suitor?"

"Suitor? I'd rather cuddle up with a baboon. In fact, a baboon would suit me better."

Rally watched the exchange as Will took a small overnight bag from the backseat and smiled down at Eunice.

Marney pulled Eunice's Sunday dress, covered with a dry cleaner bag, from the backseat, turned to Rally and shrugged. "They've been doing this for a while. They're interested in each other, but they can't quit fighting long enough to do anything about it."

Rally grinned. "I think it's sweet."

"Will," Marney called out. "Put Miss Eunice's things in the front bedroom downstairs."

Marney and Rally followed behind and listened to Eunice's barbs and Will's charming southern comebacks.

~ ~ ~ ~

Rally stood in the parlor, phone in hand. "I'll call Clay and let him know Doug's okay, at least for the moment, then I plan to have a long hot bath and get some sleep ... all night and all day tomorrow."

"No, not all day. Tomorrow's Sunday." Marney brushed past Rally on her way to hang Eunice's dress.

"Yeah, Eunice mentioned that. You all go right ahead. I'm sleeping in."

"Everyone around here goes to church on Sunday. Folks will expect to see you there. We don't want to disappoint them. Besides, you would enjoy going. We have a wonderful choir. CeCe is a soloist. When's the last time you were in church?"

"I don't care what people 'around here' think." She made air quotes with her fingers. "I'm not on public exhibition. Chicago is an expensive place to live. I pick up freelance work on weekends. Haven't been to church since ... since Kansas City."

"Well, you're not working here. You can go with us."

Rally looked at her friend and shrugged. "Besides, I didn't bring proper clothes."

"I've got plenty. Look in the closet in your bedroom. All my skinny pieces are in there. I'm sure you can find something that fits, a little out of style maybe, but no one here cares." She headed toward Eunice's bedroom.

"Dinner's in an hour. We're having roast beef. It's been cooking all day."

Rally crossed her arms. "Fine. Church in the morning, then I'm sleeping all afternoon."

Chapter 20

Rally, wrapped in a worn fleece robe borrowed from Marney, yawned for the third time as she stood in front of an open closet and sorted through clothes draped on hangers. She pressed a steaming cup of coffee to her chest. "I'd rather stay in bed."

"I heard that." Marney stopped at the open bedroom door, an iron in one hand and a coffee mug in the other. "You can take a nap after we eat. I'm making a special Sunday dinner today."

"Not on my account, I hope. I've eaten like a farm hand since I got here. I need to slow down."

"Oh, it's not because of you. We're having the pastor for dinner."

"The pastor?" Rally rolled her eyes and turned to look at her friend. "Couldn't you wait until I'm back in Chicago? Not being rude, but after all I've been through the last couple of days, I'm not too interested in having to be polite and conversational with a stranger."

"Now, don't pre-judge. He's a nice man. You'll like him. Besides, Will enjoys visiting with him." She turned her attention back to the iron in her hand and hurried down the hall.

Rally selected a straight, ankle-length brown skirt from the closet and a cream-colored turtleneck from the chest near the bed. "Lunch with the preacher? That's just great."

"You women ready?" Will's booming voice announced his entry into the house after completing the morning chores.

"We'll be ready when you are," Marney called from the laundry room. "Rally has to eat yet, but we have plenty of time."

Footsteps pounded down the hallway, but paused at Rally's room. Will stuck his head through the open door.

"You're up. We missed you at breakfast. I wanted to wake you, but Marney said to leave you be. Guess city people sleep later than country folk." He waited for a reply.

"I was up late, remember?" She yawned.

"I didn't get much more than you did. But I suspect we got more stamina. It's this clean country air, no pollutants like in the city." Will waited.

Rally walked across the room, smiled at the grizzled face, and shut the door.

"Rally, dear." Eunice Harpole's chirruping voice drifted down the hallway. "May I bother you for a moment?"

She opened the door to find Eunice decked out in a navy crepe shirt-waist dress trimmed in white lace. An older style, but it looked crisp and neat.

"You missed breakfast, dear. Marney and I made pancakes. There's still plenty of batter left. I can put on an apron and have a couple ready in no time."

"Thanks so much, Miss Eunice. That's sweet of you. Did you sleep well?"

"Not like at home, but not bad. I couldn't get to sleep from worrying about Doug. Are you sure he's safe?"

"Yes, Miss Eunice." Rally reached out and patted the older woman's arm. "Doug is okay. I'm sure Deputy Woods will get everything straightened out today, tomorrow at the latest. He'll explain when he gets things settled."

"Oh, Deputy Woods won't be doing much investigating today, that's for sure."

"Why do you say that?"

Eunice made an abrupt pivot and headed back down the hallway.

"He's the preacher."

Chapter 21

Eunice refused the front passenger seat to slip into the back with Will.

Rally got in, fastened her seat belt, and glared at Marney.

"The deputy is also the pastor. Why didn't you tell me?"

"I figured you wouldn't go to church if I told you." Marney settled into the seat next to her.

"You're right. I don't need *him* looking down at me from the pulpit. Talk about a guilt trip."

"Clay wouldn't do that. He would never try to make anyone feel guilty."

Rally backed out of the driveway and onto the road. She did a quick glance into the rearview mirror. Will and Eunice each hugged their side of the car.

"You're lookin' mighty fetchin' this morning, Miz Hargrove."

"Hmm. Thank you for noticing, but I hope you're not trying to flirt because I would not appreciate that."

"Don't worry. I only flirt with the young'uns."

Rally caught Will's eye in the rearview mirror and grinned when he winked at her.

"Uncle Will, for Pete's sake. What on earth are you thinking?" Marney looked over her shoulder at him.

"Giving Widder Hargrove something to chew on."

Marney shifted back into her seat and motioned toward the road. "Take the next right turn, then the second left. We'll be going across the dam." She looked at her friend. "Are you mad?"

Rally sat straight and stiff, her eyes on the road.

"Okay, be mad as long as you want, but you'll see. Clay's a good man, whether he's Deputy Sheriff Woods or Pastor Woods. He's fair both ways. Give him a chance, and cut me some slack, would you?"

Rally sighed. "I'm sorry, Marney. I'm not being a grateful guest. With all that's happened, it's a little hard to remember I came here to spend a nice quiet week with my best friend. The whole preacher thing is quite a shock. He kind of appealed to me, even though he threatened to give me a ticket."

"I'm sorry I didn't tell you, but I knew once you got into the church, you wouldn't get up and leave when you saw him. You wouldn't create a scene."

"No, I still have some pride. I *do* care what people, even strangers, think. Besides, I wouldn't want to embarrass you. You live here. Wouldn't want my actions to shock the good citizens of Monarch Moon and reflect on you."

She could hear Eunice and Will chatting now, neither of them interested in the front seat conversation.

"Are you attracted to Clay?"

"He's a nice-looking man. I'd have to be blind not to notice. He's pleasant, and when you can get him to smile, it's a nice one. But he's a little too uptight."

"He hasn't always been that quiet. Before Cheryl, his ex-fiancé, took off with no explanation, he glowed, laughed a lot. He wanted a future with her. Everything seemed fine on Tuesday. She left on Wednesday. Nobody knows why. All kinds of rumors floated around. Some speculated about a past she didn't want Clay to discover. I, myself, think she didn't love him like he loved her, and she didn't want marriage. He did a lot for her, took care of her, and patched up the old house she lived in. When her car broke down, he got it fixed."

"Did he know her for a long time?"

"No. She moved here from out of state. We don't know why she settled here. She said she pulled in to buy gas and fell in love with the town. She got a job as a checker at the grocery store. I never got acquainted with her. She didn't try to fit in. Quiet and distant. Nobody knew her but Clay."

"Well, I'm not planning to get involved with the deputy-slash-preacher. He's way too complicated. Like I told you, I'm attracted to him a little, but the preacher thing doesn't cut it. Besides, he deserves better." She signed. "He's a man of God. How do I measure up to those standards?"

"What do you mean, 'measure up'?"

She could sense Marney staring at her.

Rally cut her eyes back to the road. "I haven't been honest with you. You and Will could be in danger because I'm here. This isn't a vacation. It's a place to hide."

A sign pointed toward the church. She wheeled the Mustang into the parking lot.

"I'll try to explain after church."

Marney patted her hand. "I can't imagine you putting us in danger. You were always so dramatic."

Rally took a breath, looked around the parking lot, and struggled to change the conversation to something lighter. "Looks like all the country folk turned out this morning."

Marney stepped from the car and pulled the seat forward for Will. "Why the comment about 'country folk'?"

Rally nodded toward a row of nearby vehicles. "Lots of pickup trucks."

Will exited the backseat, then offered his hand to Eunice before Rally could help her from the driver's side. Eunice looked at Rally, then at Will. She scooted across the seat and took Will's hand.

"Most of the 'country folk' you're referring to are hardworking families who support themselves by farming and sometimes working part-time jobs in the area. The red Chevy crew cab over there belongs to the vet in Forsyth. The blue Dodge Ram belongs to the football coach. You don't have to be country folk to own a truck. You didn't back in Texas, either. As I remember, your daddy owned a Ford truck when we were growing up. He ranched and worked as a mechanic."

Rally leaned her head back to stare up at the tall steeple. "It seems I'm spending the morning apologizing to you, Marney. I'm cranky from lack of sleep. Please accept that excuse. I'm not like this."

"Perhaps you've gotten too citified." Marney led the way across the lawn to the old log church.

Will and Eunice trailed behind, greeting friends and neighbors. Inside, Marney headed down the red-carpeted center aisle toward the front.

"Not the front, Marney," Rally whispered. "Stop here somewhere."

"I can't. Everyone sits in the same place each week. It's been that way for generations. Families used to buy the pews they wanted and left them in their wills."

"What? You've got to be kidding."

"Shush." Marney put a finger to her lips. "I always sit near the front. Will sits toward the back with some of the older men."

They slid into a well-polished wooden pew three rows from the front. Rally admired the patina of the old oak and ached for a camera in her hands.

"Where does Eunice sit?"

"Anywhere she pleases, but most times near the front on

the left aisle. She likes to be where she can get out in a hurry if she disagrees with something Clay says in his sermon. Poor Doug follows her and takes her home."

"That's pretty rude."

"Oh, Clay's used to it. It all balances out. When she likes his sermon, she goes on about how wonderful he is."

A group of people in white choir robes walked down a side aisle toward the back of the church. An older, heavyset lady with hair too dark to be natural took her place at the organ. She wore a dress with swirls of bright green set against a purple background. A tiny purple hat with one feather sprouting out of the back sat squarely on the crown of her head. Her lipstick, thick and bold, shouted Magenta Magic.

"That's Myrna Dotson." Marney cupped a palm around her mouth. "She keeps one eye on Will and sometimes misses a note because of that distraction. I don't know what she'll do when she sees him sitting with Eunice."

Rally turned to look for the pair, then saw them sitting in a pew near the middle of the church. "Do you think she'll try to get Will to leave with her if she doesn't like the sermon?"

"Will won't budge. He loves Clay's sermons. It might be interesting to see what happens. Eunice might have to change her routine this week."

The bell in the steeple rang three times, a signal for the service to start. Everyone stood as Myrna Dotson played the introduction to "All Hail the Power." The choir sang as it moved forward from the back of the church. As it passed, Rally heard a powerful baritone voice behind them. She looked toward the sound to see Clay in a plain black robe. She couldn't pry her eyes from him as he moved up the three steps to the altar and stood behind the pulpit.

Memories flooded back as she listened to old hymns she had learned as a child. She turned toward Marney, remembering how the two of them sang their lungs out every Sunday morning, and how Jesus meant so much to them. Marney's face, bathed in the morning light streaming through the windows, took on a soft glow.

A lump swelled in Rally's throat as she watched Will and Eunice sing, oblivious to their being side lit, bathed with a spectrum of color from the stained-glass panes. Eunice's hair glowed silver in a halo of light.

The loneliness of the past few years boiled to the surface. Rally yearned for the peace and comfort she used to know before she let herself harm someone. An act that would always haunt her.

As Reverend Clay Woods ended his sermon, she clung to every word:

"Remember to be thankful for every wonderful gift the Lord has given. Keep Him in your hearts, and in your minds. If we stray, He welcomes us back. It's His promise. He doesn't leave us. It is we who leave Him."

If we stray, he welcomes us back. A tear slid down her cheek. *He doesn't leave us. It is we who leave him.*

After the benediction, the congregation joined the choir in singing the recessional hymn, "He Leadeth Me." Reverend Woods followed the choir toward the back of the church. When he looked at her, she wilted.

The congregation shook hands with the pastor and exchanged pleasantries as they exited.

Marney held Clay's hand for a moment while they exchanged greetings, and then Rally stood face to face with him. She could not make her tongue work. She only stared. Clay took her hand.

"I'm glad to see you, Rally. After the last few days, I'm sure you could use some strength. I know I sure needed it. Being here with this church family always helps me get through the next week."

"Thank you, Clay … Reverend Woods. I'm … you … I enjoyed your sermon." She could feel heat creeping up her neck and spreading into her cheeks.

"Thank you. I'll see you at Marney and Will's in a while for Sunday dinner."

"Yes, I'll be there." She withdrew her hand, turned, and hurried out the door.

People chatted in the churchyard. The elderly admired the babies. Young parents complemented the older folks on how well they looked.

Marney directed Rally's attention to a brass plaque by the door:

Christ's Church of Monarch Moon

Eli Hayes, Builder and Pastor

Built: 1867

"This church has been here a long time. The congregation had this plaque made several years ago to honor Eli and to show its history. Everyone works hard to keep it nice and in good repair."

"That's apparent. The church is spotless, and the grounds are beautiful." Rally touched the plaque, ran her hand over the logs, worn smooth by years of wind and weather.

"This Eli Hayes did a lot, huh?"

"He started this entire community, this county, beginning with the church. You should go to the museum sometime and read about him. His is quite an interesting story."

Eunice and Will waited near the Mustang while Marney introduced Rally to some of the curious churchgoers.

"Let's get on home," Will's voice carried across the churchyard. "I want out of these duds so I can enjoy Sunday dinner. Eunice said she's gonna whip up some of her sweet potato pie for us. Come on, now. You can visit another time."

The two women laughed. Marney bent her head close to Rally's. "I wonder who brought up the sweet potato pie. Will has a way about him. Poor Eunice didn't see it coming."

An old-fashioned Sunday dinner would be the first in a long time for Rally, but she wondered how it would go with Deputy-slash-Reverend Woods in attendance. She would try to avoid a conversation with him about the situation with Doug and CeCe and the mysterious happenings of the previous few days.

When they started for the car, Clay ran up to them, his robe billowing behind him.

"Marney, could you drive Will and Eunice home? I'd like to show Rally around the grounds, give her some church history."

He looked at Rally. "If you're interested. I thought you might come back and take pictures of the church and the river on the other side. It's something to see."

"Oh, no." Rally looked first at Clay, then at Marney. "No. I couldn't run off and let Marney prepare dinner by herself." She stared at her friend with her head tilted, eyebrows arched.

"It's fine, dear." Marney stretched her hand out for the keys. "You go. Clay's right. It's gorgeous over there. Take your time. We won't be eating for well over an hour." She winked at Rally. "Plenty of time."

"I'll help her," Eunice called out, "and Clay, I loved the sermon today." She shooed them off with a hand. "You two go on now. We might even get Will to set the table."

Will drew himself up to his full height. "I don't do woman's work. I've got plenty to do outside."

"Remember, Uncle. Jeb said the same thing. We know how that turned out." Marney patted him on the back.

Eunice stood on tiptoe, hands on hips, and stared up at him. "You want sweet tater pie, old man?"

"I got chickens to feed, and I gotta check on the cows."
Will squeezed into the backseat of the convertible. Marney
closed the passenger door after Eunice and waved as she
got into the car.

Rally watched the Mustang go down the gravel lane to
the road. Then Clay turned, touched her elbow, and guided
her back toward the church.

"I'll put this robe up and take care of some things.
You're welcome to come back into the church and look
around until I'm finished."

"No, I'd like to stay out here. There's a pleasant breeze
and I can smell honeysuckle. It's nice." She glanced around
the churchyard and the woods behind. "You're right. I
might come back with my camera equipment. The church
alone would make nice greeting cards."

"Don't wander too far. You've scared us once already.
Don't need you lost again."

She bristled. "I was not lost."

Clay looked down at her, his eyes soft with kindness.
"*Are* you lost, Rally?"

Startled by his question, she turned away and walked
toward the trees.

Chapter 22

C lay watched her move toward the woods behind the church. She seemed to float across the grass-covered churchyard, so graceful he wondered if she once took ballet lessons. He went back into the church and hung his vestments inside the closet with the choir robes, then took a few minutes to look around.

A wave of nostalgia swept over him as he stared at the pulpit, backlit by light filtered through the Good Shepherd carrying His lamb. Hard to believe five years had passed by so fast. When Reverend Hendrix died, he had accepted the church's invitation to fill in until they could find a permanent pastor, even though it would have to be on a part-time basis. He didn't know he would fall in love with ministering to the church. He loved being their pastor, but the church had grown in those five years, and he no longer felt adequate. Decisions were sometimes hard to make. They needed, they deserved, a full-time minister.

He took a quick look in the dressing room mirror. His

tan chinos, blue striped dress shirt and navy tie, hidden by the robe during the morning service, still looked crisp. He flicked a soft rag across his boots, grabbed his Stetson from the hat rack, took another quick look in the mirror to tilt the hat a bit, then walked out and let the door lock behind him. A few long strides brought him up with her.

They ambled along the riverbank, him pointing out watermarks left by spring floods. Some rose-bushes-gone-wild, planted early in the church history, still held faded pink summer blossoms. He loosened the tie and undid the top shirt button as they walked.

"Does the water ever get into the church?" She frowned, looked at the watermarked trees, then back at the church.

"It has, but only twice in its history. The town flooded both times. That was before the dam and the lake. Those marks from last spring are as high as it comes. You may have noticed we've walked down a gradual slope to get to the river. It takes a lot of water to get as high as the church. It won't happen again unless the dam breaks, and that isn't likely."

A clear blue stream gurgled and bounced along a multicolored rock bottom for several feet, then it widened into a deeper, quieter course. He touched her elbow, guided her along the edge, the other hand poised near her waist, ready to grab if she slipped. He could feel her resistance, but he maintained a light touch. They stopped, watched the water as he told her some church history.

"I can't tell you the number of people baptized in this water. Hundreds, thousands maybe. Eli declared the church nondenominational, a brave move in his day and time. It being the only church in the area, everyone came from miles around to worship on Sunday.

"People have turned up with baptismal certificates passed down from generations ago. One of our ladies volunteered to put together a church history book. We're hoping to publish it. We could use the money from the sales to pay for repair and refurbishing."

He knew she listened, even though he was rambling, but he understood the blue water and sky, and the splotches of orange, yellow, and red in the bushes and trees distracted her. The brilliant red sumac in front of them set the edge of the woods ablaze. He watched her eyes take mental photographs until she could return with a camera.

Her attention drifted to the cemetery across from the church, visible through the tree line.

"Are any of those stones as old as the church?"

"The oldest grave we found there is not as old as one would think. After Eli finished the church, it took a while for him to build a congregation and to find a wife. The first grave is for the infant daughter of Eli and his wife, Golden."

"Golden. Interesting name."

"As is Rally." He waited for a smile.

She ignored the remark and turned her attention back to the river. "I can't believe I didn't grab a camera out of the trunk before Marney drove away."

"Oh, no you don't. If you started today, we would miss dinner. Marney wouldn't like that." He took her arm and guided her in a broad turn.

She flinched, moved away, and walked a few paces ahead.

"What about the woods over there?" She pointed at the tree line of a thick oak forest several yards away. "Is that where Eli got the logs for the church?"

"Yes, and the story goes that the first night he camped here, he climbed deep up into those woods on the side of that mountain there—somewhere around where the cabin sets Doug took you to—and found the Monarch butterflies at roost in a huge oak tree. A bright harvest moon lit up everything and made the scene spectacular. Enraptured, he took it as a sign from God that he should build his church here in this valley."

"Was it a sign from God?"

"I like to think so." He moved a few steps to stand next to her. "The church has endured all these years. Generations have found their strength here, through wars and the Great Depression. They came here to pray together and share their faith through many tough times. During the depression, families shared what they could with their neighbors. They took care of each other. That's how it's always been." He looked down, nudged an anthill with the toe of his boot. "It's a good place to live."

"It's a delightful story. The center of this community. Such a comforting thought." She turned to stare at the woods. "Where's the tree?"

He hoped she didn't have thoughts of going into the woods on her own again.

"You mean the roosting tree?"

"Yes. Do the monarchs still come there?"

"I hope so. The migration doesn't always drift our way, but when it does, there's a kind of unwritten law that the tree, or trees, are not to be bothered during the season. We all agreed to leave the monarchs alone. It's crucial not to disturb them, so they can rest. They're on the brink of becoming an endangered species. Everyone around here plants butterfly gardens. That's why we get so many."

She focused on the dense woods, her forehead creased, her lips tightened. He could sense her wondering what it would be like to photograph such a phenomenon.

"They may be on their way to Mexico by now. I haven't seen them in a couple of days. There may be some stragglers, but I expect it's over for this year."

"This is a beautiful spot. I love the history and the story about the monarchs and Eli. Thank you for sharing them with me."

"My pleasure, Rally." He took her hand. Touched her thumb with his. "I wonder, I thought perhaps some evening we could—"

"Could do what?" She tensed. "This isn't me, Clay. You need a nice, homespun girl to darn socks, starch and iron your uniform shirts, and press your black robe every Sunday morning. I know more about the bad side of life than the good. You don't know what I've done."

"Rally. Listen." He touched her arm. "You have a good heart. I can't believe you made poor decisions on your own. Whatever hurt you've experienced, I feel sure the fault does not rest with you alone."

She brushed tears from her cheeks and pushed his hand away.

"I'm leaving in a few days. I'm going back to Chicago. There's no need to go any further with this conversation." She turned and walked back toward the church. "We'd better go. I need to help with dinner."

He watched her walk toward his truck. She needed time to heal, but time was something he didn't have.

Chapter 23

The smell of fried chicken wafted through the air to meet her as she walked through the back door. Clay, close behind, sniffed. "Man, something smells good in here."

Will greeted them in the parlor. "They're workin' on it. It's a good thing you got here when you did. If you'd been much longer, it all might've been gone. I'm starvin'."

Rally hurried through the dining room and into the kitchen, noting the place settings on the big harvest table. "Did Will do that?"

"With reluctance." Marney stood at the six-burner gas range, turning chicken sizzling in three big iron skillets.

Eunice set two fresh baked pies on wire racks to cool. "The old coot fought us about it, but we won. Marney has a way with him."

"A way with his stomach, you mean? I told him I would boil the chicken instead of frying it if he didn't help. He thinks even the devil would spit out boiled chicken."

"Sorry we're late," Rally said. "A couple came by the church right as we were leaving, saw Clay there and wanted to talk about their wedding."

"I'm not surprised. Clay never refuses his time and attention after services. He has another deputy work for him on Sunday, but the congregation knows their needs during the week will compete with his law enforcement duties. They try to catch him after church if they can. He always responds, even if it means giving up personal time and sleep."

"I figure personal time for him is nonexistent." Rally grabbed an apron and drained the potatoes. "Where's your mixer? I'll whip these bad boys up."

~ ~ ~ ~

Everyone helped carry steaming bowls and platters full of food to the table. The fried chicken melted in Rally's mouth. She couldn't put her finger on it, but something different, maybe something Marney learned here in the Ozarks, made it crunchy on the outside, tender and juicy inside. She could not refuse a third piece. A platter full at each end of the table dwindled down during the meal. She listened to small talk as bowls of mashed potatoes, cream gravy, salad, corn on the cob and sliced fresh tomatoes passed around. Then, at last, dessert.

"That's fine sweet tater pie, Miss Eunice. Best I ever ate."

Eunice looked at Will over the top of her water glass. "You'd better say something good about it. I doubt we'd be eating it if you hadn't dropped so many hints."

"Ah, Miss Eunice. You know you miss cookin' for a man."

"Yeah, you're right, for a man. Not for an ornery old possum like you."

A few chuckles rose above the mealtime clatter. All eyes

were on Will, who kept on eating his pie and didn't look up. Rally tried to refuse the piece passed to her, but she told herself she didn't want to hurt Eunice's feelings. She avoided any exchanges with Clay, and he directed his attention away from her except for passing food and offering polite, but short, comments.

Marney sat across the table. Rally could feel her watch them with interest, but she kept the conversation light.

"I suppose we could have asked your cousin Jeb to come, although he's good at showing up right at mealtime on Sunday. He knows we do this every week."

Clay took a drink of iced tea. "I'm surprised he hasn't shown up. Not like him to miss a free meal. Maybe he's catching up on the sleep he lost. I'll call him when I get home."

Eunice turned her attention to Clay. "How do you put up with that man? I know he's your cousin, but it don't mean you took him to raise. Sorry Reverend, but he's not your responsibility. I can't believe you came from the same family."

Marney looked across the table and frowned. "Thanks for speaking your mind, Miss Eunice."

Clay stopped, a bite of pie midair on his fork. He placed it back on the dessert plate, put his hands in his lap.

"Jeb possesses good qualities, Miss Eunice, even though his upbringing lacked something. His daddy was an alcoholic, and my Aunt Lizzie worked all the time to feed the kids. Jeb, being the youngest, kind of followed the rest of us around and everyone looked after him."

He dabbed at his lips with a checkered napkin.

"After Jeb's parents died, his older brothers and sisters drifted away one at a time, so I'm all that's left. I'm trying to spend time with him, bring him around. He's been coming to church, although he didn't show up today. I pray for him. I hope you all will keep him in your prayers."

"Of course we will." Marney said. Others commented

and nodded.

Rally's cell phone rang, just as she got up to take the dessert plates into the kitchen.

"Hello?" She held her breath, listened. "CeCe, what's wrong?" She looked at Clay, mouthed *Its Biggs,* then grabbed a jacket, and motioned for him to follow.

"Try to stall him. Deputy Woods is here. We'll get there as fast as we can. I hear him yelling. What does he want?"

Clay grabbed his Stetson, threw the outside door open, and Rally hurried past him. He followed her to the parking area in front of the house. They looked at the Mustang, then the cruiser, then each headed to their own vehicle.

"Stay on the phone with me." She let Clay take the lead in his truck. "We'll be there in a few minutes. If you can keep Doug from confronting him, maybe he'll give up and leave."

The truck threw gravel as Clay sped out of the driveway and down the lane toward the county road. Rally followed. "Don't let him in. We're on our way."

Gravel pelted the exterior of her treasured convertible. She imagined chip marks in the blemish-free paint job.

"Blue, if you survive Monarch Moon, Missouri, you can survive anything."

Chapter 24

CeCe paced the living room, a cell phone pressed to her ear. A half-empty pizza box sat on the coffee table next to the TV schedule.

"He's mad because last night I told him I'm having second thoughts about modeling school and what you said about living in the big city. He went off, yelled at me, and told me to stay away from you, that you are putting crazy ideas in my head and ruining my future."

The doorbell rang once, then twice more. CeCe tiptoed to the door and peeked through the diamond-shaped glass at the top. She spoke in a soft voice.

"Doug is upstairs taking a shower. As soon as he turns off the water, he'll hear Larkin carrying on and come running down here. There's going to be an awful scene. I don't know what to do."

Biggs' loud voice boomed through the door. "CeCe, open the door. It's me."

She peeked around the window curtain and watched

Larkin Biggs press a palm against the doorsill, lean into it with his head down, listening.

"I'm not feeling well." She tried to make her voice weak.

"Open up. You're not too ill to talk. It won't take a minute."

"I really don't, I can't—"

"CeCe, open this door. I'll break it down if I must. You don't want that to happen. How would you explain it to your daddy since you don't want him to know you've been seeing me? I guess you would have to blame it on your friend, Doug. Of course, that might be a good idea. I wouldn't mind seeing Paul Putnam chase him out of town."

"I'm on the phone. You'll have to wait a minute." She cupped her hand around the cell and kept her voice low. "Rally, you there? I'm right by the door. Do you hear him? He's raving like a maniac."

The sound of shattered pottery startled her. She peeked around the curtain again. Clumps of potting soil and bunches of geraniums spread out across the porch in front of the window. She moved away and backed up against the staircase.

"Your car sat in the driveway all night and it didn't leave this morning. Why didn't you go to church?"

She took a deep breath, let it out, and then another. She raised her voice. "Larkin, are you stalking me? I told you I'm not feeling well. I've got to get some rest. You need to leave."

"I heard Doug Palmer's truck went into the lake and that they haven't found him. I'm not surprised, him losing his job and all. Stinks of suicide to me."

She stiffened. "Rally, are you almost here? He's breaking things, and he's been stalking me. I'm surprised he hasn't figured out Doug is here. Please hurry."

Rally's voice broke up, but she heard her muffled answer. "Almost there. Hang on, CeCe. Keep him out …

house … Doug away."

"I'm not concerned about Palmer, just you. I thought if he's not face down in the lake, and he turns up here, you might need protection. No telling when Paul will get home. That guy wants you back. Who knows what he might try to do?"

"Larkin, for the last time, please go away. I'm on the phone with Rally. She's on her way over here."

"Marney's friend needs to mind her own business. Don't pay any attention to her. I'll get you into modeling school and even pay your expenses."

"You said there are no strings attached." CeCe paced the parquet floor. "I can't help but be concerned about your expectations of me after I get there. I can't figure out how you would benefit from doing that for me."

"C'mon, CeCe. I told you. My friend with the modeling agency is telling me he'll soon have an opening for an attractive young woman like you. He has a scholarship program for a girl with talent. I will pay your living expenses for the opportunity to be your manager. It's as simple as that."

The loud thump of footsteps bounding down the stairs caused her to jump and turn around. Doug made a leap across the room, lost his balance, banged into the wall, then landed with a thud on the floor. He squinted, shook his head, then sprang to his feet.

"Leave, Biggs. Get out of here before I make a new door with you."

"Is that Doug Palmer? What's he doing in there, CeCe? You lied to me."

"Just go, Larkin. It's none of your business why he's here. You've overstepped your bounds. I don't have to answer you, nor do I have to put up with your trying to force your way into my home. Please go."

"I'm sure your father would not be happy with that lunatic making himself at home in his house while he's down at that pharmacy working. I believe they have declared your friend in there missing, along with that woman from Chicago. Too bad they've turned up again to cause more trouble."

Doug moved toward the door with his fists doubled.

"No, Doug," she grabbed his hand. "If you hit him, you could go to jail. Besides, I think he outweighs you by thirty pounds. It wouldn't be a fair fight."

"I'm telling you, CeCe." Bigg's voice boomed. "This guy is a loser. Run him off. He's nothing but trouble."

Doug pulled his hands free from hers, danced around in front of the door with his fists clenched, his arms extended in front of his chest. "I can take him. Open that door and let me at him."

"Rally, can you hear Doug carrying on?" CeCe stood between her house guest and the door. "I'm running out of time ... and patience. I hope Clay is close."

A vehicle pulled into the driveway. She and Doug rushed to the door and watched as Officer Woods got out of his truck, looked around, settled the Stetson on his head, then walked to the front porch. He climbed the three steps and stopped in front of Larson Biggs.

"What's the trouble here?"

They watched as the interloper smiled at the deputy. "No trouble, Officer. Apparently, Miss Putnam has fallen victim to a flu bug. I was visiting with her about a few things. We may have been a little loud in our conversation. Did we disturb the neighbors?"

"You disturbed Miss Putnam," Clay said. "She made a call to a friend."

"I was just leaving when you drove up." Biggs straightened to his full height and moved away from the door. "I noticed CeCe's car in the driveway and wondered why she wasn't in church this morning. Thought I'd check on her. I'm sure you missed her lovely voice in the choir."

"We did. I was going to check on her myself. You'd best

be on your way now. I'll see if she needs anything."

A sneer spread across Biggs' face, exposing straight white teeth. He nodded to the deputy, backed down the steps from the porch and started toward his car parked against the curb. He stopped and looked back.

"By the way, Deputy. Doug Palmer is in there with CeCe. I'm concerned about her safety. It's a strange thing, driving his truck into the lake like that, don't you think? Perhaps he should be on suicide watch." He tapped his finger against his pursed lips.

"You know, Deputy, he may have been the one who shot into my cabin. He's blaming me for CeCe's dumping him." He flicked his hand as though swatting a fly.

"Strictly her choice, of course, but jealousy can make young men do strange things. I've done nothing more than encourage her to pursue a career."

Bigg's face sobered. "I'm expecting some answers about that incident. I need to know who tried to shoot me. If you don't do something soon, I may have to speak to a higher authority about your work—or lack of—Deputy Woods."

"I'm workin' on it, Biggs. In the meantime, you stay out of trouble."

Clay walked to the edge of the porch and straightened to his full height. He stood there until Biggs' car was down the street and out of sight.

CeCe turned from the doorway and looked at Doug. "You've got to leave. If he's the one who's after you, he'll know where you are. If he isn't, he'll spread the word all over town and whoever *is* after you will come here."

"That's why I can't leave you alone. There's no telling who might be sneaking around. We're both leaving. The only place I know that might be safe is Will's."

"There's the cabin."

"No, I'm not taking you to the cabin anymore. If it got around that we were there together, the whole town would be gossiping. It's risky enough that I stayed overnight at your house. We'll have to talk to Rally and Clay. They can take you to Will's. I'll go back to the cabin or find somewhere else to hide."

"I don't want you to be alone. Maybe Clay can put you in jail overnight. That might be the safest place for you under the circumstances."

"I've never been in jail in my life, and today's not the day to start. I'll take my chances."

"CeCe might be right. Jail could be the best option." They turned to see Clay standing in the doorway. He looked across the street and nodded at the blue Mustang pulling up to the curb.

"For now, CeCe, you need to go with Rally back to Will's place. That seems to be the safe house this week. They've been kind and hospitable to everyone. I'm sure they'll welcome you as well."

CeCe looked at Doug. "Where will *you* go?"

"I don't know, maybe Clay's right. He certainly has enough reason to lock me up. A kidnapping charge may be what keeps me alive." Doug stared out the window and watched Rally rush across the lawn toward them.

Chapter 25

"Sorry I missed the fun." Rally walked into the house, then went straight to CeCe.

"I took a wrong turn. Are you okay?"

"We'll have to tell my dad." Tears welled in the young woman's eyes. "He should know the complete story. He lives in this house too, and someone could mistake him for Doug. I don't want him to be hurt because of me. This is my fault. I've been so stupid."

Doug gathered CeCe into his arms. "No, you can't blame yourself. Biggs is a smooth talker. Who could blame you for wanting to have an exciting career?"

He released her and looked into her eyes. "You're beautiful enough to be a movie star, let alone a model."

Rally and Clay looked at each other. The deputy motioned toward the door, then followed Rally to the porch.

"Why don't you take CeCe out to spend the rest of the day with Will and Marney? I'm sure Miss Eunice is getting restless by now, and she loves CeCe. It will give her someone new to fuss over. I'll take Doug with me. I can make sure he's safe."

"No," she shook her head. "I'd rather you drop CeCe off at Will's. I think it's time for me to meet the pharmacist. He needs to know what's going on, but I don't think CeCe is in any shape to explain to him right now. Doug wanted me to talk to him. You know what they say, there's no time like the present."

Clay looked back into the house at the embracing couple, then back at Rally. "You're sure you want to do that?"

"Yeah." Her eyes welled up. "A father-daughter relationship is special. He should realize the treasure he has and do right by her."

The deputy called out as Rally walked across the street to her car. "Keep an eye out for Biggs. I'm afraid he could be dangerous."

"I've met worse." Rally gave him a dismissive wave, then slid into the driver's seat and pulled away from the curb.

~ ~ ~ ~

Late afternoon sun highlighted the brilliant red in the maple trees lining South Maple Street. Rally turned into a Speedy Mart convenience store and pulled up to the gas pumps. An out-of-order note hung from the card reader, anchored on one end with duct tape. She grabbed her billfold from her purse. Dried red leaves crunched under her boots as she walked across the lot.

"Looks like your reader is out of order."

"That so?" A rotund, middle-aged man swiped her card and handed it back. "Well, maybe in another twenty years, if you grace us with your presence again, it'll be fixed. They're slow as molasses getting those things repaired."

She took her card from him and turned to go, but reconsidered.

"I wasn't trying to be smart. I'm sure you heard about that reader all day. At least this is a small town, with not as much traffic as Chicago. I hate Chicago."

"Apology accepted. I don't like Chicago either. I retired from my job there and moved down here. You should think about that yourself."

"Maybe I should." She walked back out and started pumping gas into the car.

"Well, if it isn't Miss Troublemaker."

Larkin Biggs stood on the other side of her car. A smug smile stretched across his face. She glanced around the parking lot and recognized the black SUV she had seen at the Putnam house, the same one that had followed Doug out of town before his truck ended up in the water.

Maybe she should have told Clay she recognized the vehicle before she left him at CeCe's. Too late now, but she could call him as soon as she got rid of Biggs.

He moved closer. Close enough to make her uncomfortable. She felt clammy perspiration forming around her hairline.

"We've not officially met. I'm Larkin Biggs." He stuck out his hand.

"No, we haven't." She tightened her grip on the gas nozzle, the only weapon within reach. She ignored his hand and took her time looking him over. Piercing green eyes looked straight into hers. Glossy dark hair, gray streaked at the temples, shimmered in the sun like the back of a black widow spider. He was handsome, in a sinister way. He reminded her of a vampire from a horror flick. The pump clicked, shattering her concentration.

"Looks like I'm done here."

She held the nozzle, reluctant to let go. Even though the man towered over her, she did not move away but stood her ground. He was close enough she could not ignore the rippling muscles under a white Oxford shirt, the broad shoulders, and trim waist of a bodybuilder. She brushed tousled strands of hair out of her face and stood firm.

"That's right. I believe you *are* through here, and finished with whatever business you have in Monarch Moon." He smiled through tight-clenched lips. "I suggest you find a reason to leave early. You've caused too much trouble already."

She pointed the nozzle at his face, the scent of gasoline vapor in the air.

"CeCe deserves better than you. I've figured out your scheme, Biggs. I know why you're so desperate to lure her away. You don't want to help her go to modeling school any more than you want to buy Miss Eunice's trailer park. You had to act as though you wanted other property to keep the spotlight off your interest in something more valuable. CeCe." She glared at him.

"It's obvious you have a wild imagination and are making things up to discredit me." Biggs pushed the nozzle away from his face. "I want to help this town by building a lovely development of upscale homes on the lake that will draw people into the area. The town will prosper." He grinned. "The community will thank me."

"And who profits from that? You're a liar and a leech. You want to lure her away, try to talk her into marrying you, and if that doesn't work, you'll use whatever means it takes to control her so that you can then manage her wealth when she turns twenty-one. She's a sweet kid. I won't let you do that."

Biggs drew in a deep breath, straightened, and locked his eyes on her.

"You are really annoying me. I'll not have you spouting off to the community with such tales. It could ruin business for me. My interest in CeCe is platonic. She is a beautiful young woman and can go far. I like to mentor young people, get them started in life."

A car honked behind them. A man yelled out of the driver's window. "Hey, ma'am. If you're finished, please move on."

Rally placed the nozzle back on the hook, secured the gas cap, and opened the car door. She turned to get into the driver's seat, but paused and stared back at Biggs.

"Don't threaten me, Larkin Biggs. I will not leave Monarch Moon one minute sooner than I planned because of you or anyone else. And, before I leave, I promise you, Paul Putnam will know what a jerk you are and what your plans are for his daughter."

Once inside the car, she dug in her purse for her cell phone. Biggs walked to the back of the Mustang, stood, and looked at the bluebonnets painted above the rear fender, then walked around to the passenger side of the car. As Rally punched Clay's number, Biggs' face loomed in the open window.

"That's quite a lovely touch, the little blue flowers back there. It would be a shame to see your precious little convertible meet the same fate as Palmer's red pickup."

He turned, started toward the SUV, then looked back.

"By the way, we never had this conversation. I will deny every word, then turn you into an idiot in the eyes of this town. Don't mess with me either, Rally Chandler. I wonder what folks would think if they found out you were in a deserted cabin all night with Doug Palmer. I suppose I could find out a lot more about you if I put my mind to it. Better leave it alone, my dear." He turned and sauntered off toward his car.

Blood pulsed in her neck. The heat moved into her face. She touched the scar over her carotid artery, then got out of the car and slammed the door behind her. She thought about newspaper headlines and threats made by a madman.

"Biggs! Turn around and look at me. I don't want you to miss any of this."

He made a slow turn to face her. The grin still plastered

across his rock-hard face.

She stood, her spine straight, feet shoulder width apart, hands on her hips.

"First off, I'm not your *dear*." She spat the word out of her mouth. "Second, a lot scarier than you have threatened me. Third, a few days ago, I wouldn't have cared what people around here thought of me. I was only concerned with myself. But now that I see what a nasty weasel you are, I plan to tell everyone I see what a low life they've had hanging around their beautiful little town, and I hope they run you out before the sun goes down tomorrow. Tonight would be even better. I've learned from your selfishness, Biggs. I never want to be anything close to the likes of you."

She got into the Mustang and backed away from the pump, coming close enough to Larkin Biggs to make him jump back. She glanced into her rearview mirror. He stood next to his car, still watching her.

Traffic picked up as Rally headed down Maple Street toward Main and to the pharmacy. She couldn't stop her hand from shaking the cell phone as she tried to explain to Clay what had transpired.

"He threatened me, Clay. He knew my last name, and that Doug and I were at the cabin together. How did he know that?"

"He probably heard someone mention your name during a conversation. As far as you and Doug being at the cabin together, I hate to say it, but Will has a hard time not spilling the beans. He gossips with the older men around, or maybe it was Jeb. He likes to share information as well. However, Biggs may not be making idle threats. You'll have to be on guard until I can get enough on him to lock him up. Will you sign a complaint against him?"

"Clay, it's my word against his. He's smooth. He can make people believe him. Even more reason to make Paul Putnam aware of the vulnerability of his daughter, how much she needs him."

"Maybe you'd better get off the streets and head back to Will's place. You can talk to Paul in the morning."

"So, I'm hiding from Biggs? Maybe you should put me in jail with Doug. You can always give me a delayed ticket for running you off the road. Or you could make me an accomplice to my kidnapping, or hiding a fugitive, my kidnapper. I'm sure you can come up with something."

"Oh, come on, Rally." Clay's voice sounded strained, irritated. "I'd rather put you in jail than see you harmed, but I don't have a reason to hold you against your will."

"I'm sorry, Clay. It's been a rough day, but I need to finish what I started. I think CeCe knows what Biggs is now, but she needs a better relationship with her dad. She deserves that, and he needs to get straightened out about a few things."

"All right, but you call me every half hour. I want to know where you are and what you're doing. If you don't call me, I'll call you."

"Good enough. I'm almost at the pharmacy now. I'll let you know what happens."

Rally pulled into the alley. The pharmacy sat in the center of the block. She parked in a loading zone in the next block down from the back entrance when she recognized Jeb's old truck parked at the back of the store. Spooked by her encounter with Biggs, she determined to approach the pharmacy with caution. Jeb made her uncomfortable, especially after what Clay told her about the footprints.

Darkness crept in and made trash bins, loose containers, and empty soda bottles hard to see. A few stores down, a single back door light cast shadows across the paved surface. She stepped on an empty plastic bottle that rolled from under her foot and hit a metal trash bin a few feet away. Out of the shadows, a cat scurried toward Rally. Feline and human jumped at the same time. The cat darted back into the shadows. The human clutched her chest and watched the animal disappear behind a storage building across the alley.

Maybe this was not such a good idea with Jeb there, but perhaps he would leave soon. She cracked the door open, listened, then heard voices coming from the office. She reached up and cupped the bell in her hand and entered. Curious, she slipped through the aisles until she could hear the conversation. The office door was ajar. She recognized Jeb's voice and another that she assumed was Paul Putnam's.

"You're crazy. What are you doing, bringing that shotgun in here? I can't believe you shattered Biggs' window and tore a hole in his ceiling with that thing. You were supposed to scare him a little when he was out somewhere alone, not at the resort. They could accuse you of attempted murder."

Rally bent low and slid behind the soda fountain to get a better look. Jeb stood in front of Putnam, holding the gun.

"He didn't get hurt. I was gonna shoot up in the air, thought that would shake him up, but a leaky hose in the flowerbed spilled under the window and created mud. I slipped in it and the gun went off."

The two men continued to argue as she retreated to the back door. She pulled her cell phone out of her hip pocket to report to Clay, but a few bars of "Clair de Lune" signaled an incoming call. She stuck it under her jacket to muffle the sound.

The discussion in the office stopped. The entire pharmacy went snowfall quiet. Rally urged the back door open, but she forgot about the bell. This time, it sounded like Big Ben.

"Someone's out there. Stay in here until I see who it is. Don't look out the door. I don't want anyone to associate us and say something to your cousin. I'll be right back."

The Mustang seemed a mile away. She ran to the

darkened loading zone, crawled into the car, and waited. Paul Putnam walked into the alley and looked both ways, then went back inside. Afraid he might have seen her, she didn't waste time getting onto the street and out of town.

"Clay. You will not believe what I saw and heard. Where can we meet?"

Chapter 26

Rally looked around the jail and saw things that looked too familiar, things that she thought were far behind her. The past rushed up to hit her in the face, flashbacks of handcuffs, cells with bars, interrogation rooms, and bloodstains on a white shirt.

Clay turned and looked at her but continued his conversation with the dispatcher.

"Tell Adams to go by Putnam's Pharmacy. Pick up Paul Putnam and if Jeb Andrews is still there, bring him along. They have a gun, so be careful. If Jeb isn't there, have someone track him down. I want them in here together."

He gave a description of Jeb's truck, then turned his attention to Rally, who stared at Doug in his cell.

"Are you okay?" Clay motioned for her to sit in a chair by his desk.

"Oh, sure. I'm fine. A little nervous. Let's see, threatened by a lunatic at a convenience store, a narrow escape from being shot in a pharmacy." She nodded her head. "Yeah, I think I'm good."

"I doubt Jeb would shoot at you. Shooting someone isn't something he would do on his own. I'm sure Paul Putnam wouldn't want that to happen either. I'm wondering why he would have Jeb try to scare Biggs."

Doug got up from the cot, opened his cell door, and walked out. He pulled a straight-backed chair across the room and set it in front of Rally's, then straddled it backwards.

"Looks like neither of us can stay out of trouble. Maybe I should bust out of this joint so I can protect both you and CeCe. I'd like to get a crack at that Biggs guy. He's messed up a lot of lives in the short time he's been here."

"After what I saw and heard at the pharmacy, Biggs isn't the only threat." Rally stared back at him. "Jeb's running around with a gun, and Paul Putnam evidently hired him to scare Biggs away. He must have found out about CeCe seeing him. I hope he hasn't paid Jeb to come after you, too."

"I plan to find out." Clay stood by Rally's chair. "Dispatch said Adams picked Paul Putnam up at the pharmacy. He was getting ready to leave. Paul told Adams that Jeb had left a few minutes before him. They're on their way in. We'll find out what's going on when they get here. In the meantime, I've got people looking for Jeb."

Rally watched Clay's face, saw the sadness and hurt in his eyes.

"I never thought warning fellow officers about my cousin would ever happen, that he's armed and possibly dangerous. I know in my heart he's no threat, but it's my duty to do everything in my power to protect law enforcement personnel, as well as the public." He shook his head.

"You're not responsible for Jeb. He made his own choices." Rally reached out and touched his arm. "You can't blame yourself for what he's done."

"That's just it. I'm not sure what he's done. I suspected Jeb had something to do with some house burglaries that happened a few months ago. When I was looking around his place after I matched up the footprints at Marney's and the Crest View Motel, I discovered why he left the ATV in the driveway. That outbuilding he used for a garage is full of everything from television sets to diamond rings. I don't believe he stole the stuff, but I think he's fencing it, selling it outside the area. I'm keeping track of him, hoping he leads us to the rest of the gang."

"So, the footprints matched." Rally nodded. "That goes along with what I heard Jeb and Paul discussing. I'm so sorry, Clay. I know you hate to arrest your own cousin, but he made decisions that have left you with no choice. You must do what you're sworn to do."

"I know. There's no question about that. Still, in a lot of ways, I feel like I've failed him." He walked to the desk and picked up the keys to the cruiser.

"Failed him?" Rally stood. "Clay, he's a grown man. He's not a kid anymore. He must take responsibility for his actions. You haven't failed him, he's failed you."

The deputy looked at her, combed his hair with his fingertips, and settled the Stetson back on his head.

"You're a kind woman, Rally." He looked at Doug, then back at her.

"Do you two think you can stay out of trouble while I help look for Jeb? I want to pull Larkin Biggs in here as well. I found a patch of muddy grass out at the lake where Doug's truck went in. Tire tracks there look like they match the tread on his SUV."

Doug jumped up and followed Clay. "Take me with you. If it was Biggs that pushed my truck into the lake and tried to drown me, I want a chance at him."

"No way, Doug. I'd like this to be as peaceful as possible. I don't need you to start a fight and maybe give him a chance to get away or get hurt yourself. You stay here with Rally and keep her company until I get back. Adams should be here with Paul any minute."

The two jail guests watched the deputy walk out of the office.

"When they finish what they're going to do with Paul, maybe that will be a good time for me to talk to him about CeCe," Rally said.

"Well, he'll be a captive audience, that's for sure." Doug grinned.

"Really, Doug?" She stared.

"Hey, I was just joking. I never thought Paul was a bad guy, even when he didn't want me dating CeCe. I knew he was trying to protect her. He wanted better for her. I can't blame him for that."

"Give yourself a break, Doug. You're a great guy. Any girl would be lucky to have you."

"You think so?"

"I know so."

"So, after you've talked to Paul, how about you and me get out there and see what we can do to help find Biggs? The more folks looking, the better chance of finding him."

A mischievous smile spread across Rally's face. "You may be right."

Chapter 27

O fficer Denzil Adams escorted Paul Putnam into the station. He motioned for the pharmacist to sit down in a straight chair, while he settled into the big ergonomic model behind the desk, then thumbed through papers on a clipboard.

"Well, I've read your rights, explained why you are being detained, and went through all this other stuff with you. You want to call anybody?"

Doug walked over to the desk. "Good grief, Denzil. Paul Putnam is no criminal. He's the pharmacist, for Pete's sake. The only one in town, I might add. Better stop and think about the next prescription you need filled. He might not be in any hurry to do it for you. You might have to go to the next town—"

"Oh, hi, Doug. Clay said you'd be here, you and that city gal. What's her name?" Adams looked up from his paperwork.

Rally approached the desk. "Rally, my name is Rally

Chandler."

"Yeah, well, the best thing for you two to do is stay out of the way. I'm following procedure. Doing what the county pays me to do."

Paul Putnam sat in the chair, subdued, looking first at Rally, then Doug.

"Doug, I need to apologize. I blamed you for CeCe not going back to school, for wanting her to stay in town so you could be with her, and maybe even marry her. I wanted her to get away from here, get an education, see what life is like somewhere else, not wish too late for something different."

"And not marry below her level?" Doug slumped into his chair.

"No, that's not what I meant. I want her to be happy, find the right person, whoever that might be. I want her to have what her mother and I shared." Paul lowered his head.

Rally dragged her chair closer to him. She waited a minute before she spoke.

How deeply do I go into this?

"Mr. Putnam … may I call you Paul?"

He nodded.

"I would like to talk to you about CeCe. She shared some things with me. This isn't a great time, and it may be painful for you, but I feel it's important we talk. You may hate me when I'm through, but I'm leaving anyway, so …"

The pharmacist raised his head and looked at her. Doug engaged Officer Adams in conversation so Rally could speak openly.

"First, you need to know that your daughter loves you so much. She would do anything for you. You also need to know that she is painfully lonely. You lost your wife, but she lost her mother and her grandmother, a grandmother who filled the gap that you and your wife may have created. CeCe told me that the two of you were so absorbed in your relationship, there was no room for her. She envied your love. She wanted so much to be a part of it, but you didn't let her in."

Tears trickled down Paul's face. He pulled a handkerchief from his hip pocket and wiped them away.

"CeCe doesn't know. She doesn't realize that her mother almost died having her. I prayed and prayed that if God would let her live, I would devote my life to her, take care of her, and be everything she needed. When she came through, I was intent on keeping my promise. She used to tell me she was afraid she wouldn't love me back as much as I loved her. She tried so hard to split her time equally between CeCe and me, but she never was well." He stared at the floor.

"After a while, Elinor, Karen's mother, took over caring for CeCe. I think she started doing it mostly to relieve the stress on Karen, but after a time, her granddaughter was her pride and joy. She adored CeCe."

Rally looked across the office at Doug, still chatting with Deputy Adams.

"Paul, I don't think God wants us to make those kinds of promises. You put too much pressure on yourself, and by doing that, you put pressure on Karen. I don't have any experience of my own yet, but it seems to me a baby takes a lot of time and care. You were lucky to have Karen's mother."

"I know all of that now, but it's too late to change things. After Karen died, CeCe had her grandmother, but I had no one. I felt so alone." Tears broke loose. He sobbed. "I miss her terribly."

"And your daughter misses you, Paul. She needs you. She doesn't have anyone, either. You need each other. That's the way it should be. You're her father. You've got to reach out to her before she builds a wall between you."

She reached into her purse, and handed him a pack of tissues.

"Don't you see why Biggs made such an impression on

her? He offered a fun career, a new life, fame, and fortune. It was all a lie, of course, but young women starved for attention believe that kind of deception.

"I'll tell you another thing. She could do a lot worse than Doug Palmer. He has a good heart, and he loves CeCe. He wants to go to nursing school and share his life with her, right here in Monarch Moon. I'll agree. He takes a little getting used to, but he's a good guy. Give him a chance. You both want what's best for her."

"Rally, quick, over here." Doug stood in front of the door, wind-milling his arm to get her attention.

"What on earth?" Rally hurried over to the door and looked up and down the street.

"It's Biggs. I saw him drive by here. He's turning left at the corner. Let's go."

Officer Adams shoved the chair away from the desk, turning it over. "You stay here. I'll pursue him. He won't get far. I'll notify Deputy Woods."

"Sorry Denzil, we're doing this one." Doug grinned and winked at Rally. "You got a dangerous criminal to book. You'd be neglecting your duty if you left him here alone. Rally and I are out of here."

They hurried down the steps to the parking lot where the blue Mustang waited.

"Tell me I'm not crazy," Rally yelled as she jumped into the driver's seat and started the engine.

"You're not crazy." Doug folded his long legs into the car and slammed the door as Rally sped into the street and headed west.

Chapter 28

Rally steered Blue through the residential area behind the sheriff's department until she came to Missouri Route 13. Doug pointed for a left turn, his eyes on the black SUV as it disappeared in the distance. He pounded a fist on the dashboard.

"Calm down!" She reached out, flattened his hand with her own.

"But, he's running." He pushed her hand away. "I knew it. He came by, saw your car in the parking lot, and figured they'd be after him. Turn left at the stop sign. He's going to Crest View to collect his things, or he's on his way straight out of town."

She brushed the hair away from her face as they coursed down the farm-to-market road at twenty miles per hour over the posted speed limit, her eyes fixed on the road ahead.

"Things are coming together," she said. "Biggs wanted you out of CeCe's life, so he followed you to the lake, caught you asleep in the truck and banged you on the head with something hard enough to knock you out. He got the brake off and shifted your truck into neutral. By giving a little push with that big old SUV, it rolled right into the water."

"Yeah, and when they found me, if they found me, the bump on my head and my truck in the water would probably be explained away as an accident caused by careless driving on my part."

Rally stared at the directional road signs ahead. "Which way?"

"Make a left at this next turn." Doug pressed a palm into the dash to brace himself as she wheeled around the corner.

"But don't you think they would consider foul play?" She straightened the car.

"You said you watched me storm out of the pharmacy," Doug said. "How many others do you think saw that?"

"Biggs saw you, that's for sure. I saw him following you out of town. There was traffic, and there were several people walking along the sidewalk." She leaned forward and scanned the road. "You sure we haven't lost him?"

"I'm sure. There's no place he can go except straight ahead." He leaned back in his seat. "Let me ask you this. What was your impression that first time you saw me at Putnam's?"

She glanced up at the headliner. "Let's see. Reckless, maybe a little rude. You bumped into me and didn't even say excuse me." She sensed him shift in the seat and look straight at her.

"So, answer me honestly. Would you think it a stretch of the imagination that I ran my truck into the lake and drowned?"

"I don't know. I hope someone would question it, though."

Doug pointed ahead. "There he is. He topped the hill ahead of us. We're gaining on him. Won't this thing go any faster?"

"I'm going as fast as I dare. I won't take a chance on wrecking this car. It's the last thing my dad gave me. It was my high school graduation present."

"I can't blame you for that. Maybe we should have left this for Clay to tackle."

She jerked her head around and nailed him with a look. "So *now* you're having second thoughts? Maybe I should give Clay a call and tell him to drop everything and hurry over here because we think Biggs is leaving town, and we decided we ought to chase him a bit. Ya think?"

"No!" He scrunched down in his seat. "Besides, Clay's busy looking for Jeb. I'm sure there's more to that story."

"Yeah, I expect Jeb's the one who told Paul that Biggs was spending time with CeCe. The poor guy must have thought he was battling both of you. It's sad that he was so miserable. I hope they take it easy on him. I don't think he intended to hurt anyone. He was being protective of his daughter."

"Left, Rally. Quick!" He pulled on his seatbelt to loosen it and sat on the edge of the seat. "He turned left on that side road. He's trying to ditch us. I know a road that crosses that one. We can cut him off there."

"And how do you propose we do that? Do you plan to stand in the middle of the road and try to wave him down? He would mow right through you."

"I was thinking we could block it. Maybe turn the car sideways so he can't get around."

Rally turned to stare at him. "Are you insane?" She shook her head. "No, I'm going to call Clay. They're equipped for roadblocks. They have those things with spikes on them to throw out in the road … don't they? You can tell him about the cutoff road. We're not doing that with my car."

She pointed at the backseat. "Grab that purse and get my phone. Call Clay, put it on speaker, and hold it close." She caught Doug rolling his eyes. "Please." He did as she instructed.

"Clay, Rally here. We're in pursuit of Biggs off Highway 13. He's leaving town. No doubt about it. I'm going to let Doug explain where we are. Hold on."

Doug moved the phone away from Rally's face and cut the speaker. "He's trying to lose us by going cross-country on County Road BB, but you can intercept him by cutting across on that old road through the state park. Yeah, we'll meet you there." He slipped the cell phone back into Rally's purse.

"Okay, keep going straight. We're close. We can park at the side of the road and watch the action. Clay says he's not far."

"He doesn't have a problem with us chasing Biggs?"

"Oh yeah, he has a problem with it. He threatened to lock us both up for interfering with police business."

"Can he do that?"

"I don't know, but I think so. I've been to jail once today. Not looking forward to a second time." He grimaced. "Turn onto the next gravel road up here. It will intersect Biggs' route."

When she found the side road, she wheeled around and backed into it. She let the car idle and turned to look down the road.

"How close was Clay? Shouldn't he be here by now?"

"He should be along any time." He focused on the road to the left of them. "Here comes Biggs. He topped that first hill. Whoa. He's not worried about the speed limit either. Clay had better hurry. If he doesn't, we'll have to intercept him ourselves."

She glared at him. "Not with my car. If you want to stop him, get out there and wave him down, but I'm having no part of it." She crossed her arms over the steering wheel and leaned forward.

"Come on, Rally, he's getting closer, and he's moving

fast. Get out there, now. Remember, he threatened you, and think about what he tried to do to CeCe. If he gets past us, he'll make it to I-44, and it will be twice as hard to catch him."

"Isn't that what they use those all points bulletins for? Wouldn't the Highway Patrol chase him down?"

Doug slapped the dashboard with his hand. "Rally, we have him now. At least we can get behind him if he gets around us. I'll bet when he sees your car in the intersection, he'll turn down this road and run smack into Clay. Let's go!" He was bouncing in his seat.

Biggs' car topped the second hill and bore down on the crossing. Rally bit her bottom lip, then threw the Mustang into drive. Gravel pinged against metal as she floored the accelerator and pulled into the road.

"I'm sorry, Daddy. This is for a good cause … I hope." Fear glued her palms to the steering wheel.

As the Mustang shot into the crossroad, the SUV hit the top of the hill above them. She heard Doug gasp at the same time she slammed the brake pedal with her booted foot. The car skidded sideways on the loose gravel, but she stayed in control and turned the car across the road, where it sputtered and died. Two frantic attempts to restart failed.

"This isn't happening." She reached across Doug, threw open the glove box, and retrieved the Beretta.

Doug's eyes widened. He jabbed an index finger into his chest. "Don't point that thing at me."

"Take it. It's loaded. We have little time. Get out and go stand in the road."

"No way! I've only shot deer, rabbit, that kind of stuff." He stared at her, his mouth open. "I've never shot a person before."

She rolled her eyes. "You don't shoot him, just the tire. Cause a blowout." She pushed the gun in his hand.

"That peashooter wouldn't put a dent in that much rubber. Besides, the accuracy would be too iffy."

"Then go for the passenger side windshield. It might crack all the way across and distort his vision, plus scare the daylight out of him. He's bound to lose control." She looked back up the road at the SUV. "Move it. He's not slowing down."

"No way! I'm not doing that. Just leave the car on the road. He'll have to take the ditch and lose control." Doug leaned forward to look around Rally. "He's bearing down on us while we argue. My vote is, let's bail out of here, just in case."

Her eyes widened. "And let him plow into Blue and tear the heck out of her? I'm not giving him the pleasure."

The black SUV charged toward them with no sign of slowing. She chewed her bottom lip, pulled the gun from Doug's trembling hand, then threw the door open and jumped out. She settled her hips against the front fender, spread her feet shoulders-width apart. Aimed. Faltered.

A prayer slipped through her lips as she lowered the gun and dropped it on the ground. *Lord, I don't want to go through that again. Please make him stop.*

She could see Biggs' face pale as he pulled the steering wheel to the right. The SUV fishtailed, turned, then headed back down the road. She felt her heart thump in her ears.

"Are you okay?" Doug peeked up over the hood on the opposite side of the Mustang.

A loud thud and a noisy crunch of metal drew their attention.

A whitetail buck trotted across a field, unscathed. The front end of the SUV embraced a large oak tree. The rear end rested in the ditch.

"I think so. That was close." She gave Doug a quick once-over. "You sure got out of there fast."

"A woman with a gun makes me nervous."

"It does me too. I'm just glad he swerved."

Strains of "Clair de Lune" emitted from her cell phone.

"Want me to get it?" Doug said.

"No." She walked backwards toward the noise. "I've got—"

A sheriff's cruiser pulled up beside the wrecked vehicle.

Deputy Sheriff Clay Woods, gun drawn, walked around the side of the SUV to the front, negotiating the ditch.

"I didn't see Biggs crawl out of there, did you? I hope he's not armed." Doug walked to the rear of the Mustang and stared down the road.

"Now, you worry." Rally shook her head.

He nodded. "I did before. I considered an attempt to stop you when you jumped out there like Wonder Woman, but like I said, a woman with a gun scares me."

Deputy Woods opened the driver's side door and motioned for Biggs to get out. Rally had not thought about the danger of his job, but watching him go through all the protocol for securing a prisoner made her realize his life was on the line every time he put on a uniform. She thought she was on the verge of hero worship.

Doug's voice filtered in with her thoughts.

"Since I'm an emergency medical technician, I'm obligated to run on down there. You need to sit in the car for a few minutes. You're too shaky to drive."

"Um, yeah. I may never drive again. Go on, I'm fine. I don't want to face Clay right now. I'm sure he's not happy with us."

In the few minutes it took Doug to run down the road, Clay was guiding Biggs out of the ditch toward the cruiser.

She heard Doug call out, "Do you want me to check him for injuries, Deputy?"

"He's okay, a little shaken up maybe. I'll take him over to Hayes Memorial and have him checked out at the E.R."

Rally turned the car around and drove to the other vehicles. She pulled over on the side of the road and watched as another cruiser pulled alongside the first.

Sheriff Bill Turner got out, stretched, and looked at the scene in front of him. His snug uniform shirt gaped between the buttons. A fringe of gray hair was visible under a tan Western hat. His voice boomed through the still afternoon.

"Is this that guy you were after, Deputy?" The sheriff watched Clay guide Biggs out of the ditch, his wrists handcuffed.

"It's good to see you back, Sheriff. Yep. This is the guy. How was your vacation?"

Sheriff Turner nodded. "It was okay. Too many in-laws, too much time at the Grand Canyon. Not a good way to recover from knee surgery. I sat in a lodge while they all played tourist. I have no complaints about being left behind." He shook his head.

"Doug thinks a deer ran across the road and caused the accident. I suspect Biggs of hitting Doug on the head and pushing his truck in the lake."

The sheriff looked at Doug, then down the road to Rally and the Mustang.

"What's going on here?" He limped around the cruiser and motioned for Biggs.

"A little unfinished business, Sheriff. I need to visit with these two would-be vigilantes."

"I'll take care of your prisoner, then. You handle your unfinished business. I'll see you back at the jail."

Doug and Clay walked to the Mustang. Her first thought was to take off and leave Doug to explain, but she was as much to blame as he was. Clay had told them to stay out of it, but they had disobeyed an officer of the law. She got out of the car and stood by the door.

Sheriff Turner pulled around the two men. She moved closer to Blue as he came parallel to her car. The sheriff tipped his hat, smiled, and nodded. Larkin Biggs sat in the back seat, staring through the side window. For a split second, his piercing green eyes connected with hers. She felt them burn into her. She stared back.

Not this time. I'm through hiding.

She watched the cruiser until it disappeared. When she turned around, Doug and Clay were standing behind her.

"You're pale as bleached bones." Clay touched her shoulder. "Did that creep say something to you?"

Rally leaned against the side of the Mustang for support. "No, but I don't think he likes me."

Chapter 29

Jeb Andrews sat on the cot earlier occupied by Doug and ate chili from Marie's Diner. Rally grinned when Deputy Adams jumped up, brushed crumbs from his mouth, and hurried around the desk when they walked in. An almost empty bowl of chili and a box of saltines sat next to the telephone. The officer nodded toward Jeb.

"The town marshal found him walking across the dam in the pedestrian lane. That old truck of his pooped out on the other side. He's been singin' like a spinning top. Told all about how Paul Putnam had him spying on CeCe, found out she was seein' Biggs and hired him to scare Biggs out of here." The deputy stuck his thumbs in his belt and thrust out his chest, as though he had caught the perp himself. Adams rushed on, sparing no details.

"He admitted the shotgun in his truck came from the stolen stuff in his outbuilding, said Putnam didn't know where it came from and really wasn't in favor of him using it, but that he convinced him it would be effective." Adams stopped, took a deep breath, then rambled on.

"He's come clean and named the thieves that brought him the stolen articles to fence. I think Jeb's telling the truth. We've got surrounding law enforcement officers out looking for them now."

Jeb set the chili bowl on the floor as Clay walked to the cell.

"Is there anything you want to say to me, Jeb?"

"Well, cuz." Jeb stared at his feet, avoiding eye contact. "I screwed up. You know I've been out of work a long time and needed money."

With arms crossed, Clay looked at him for a moment. "You're going to jail for sure this time. You know that, right?"

Jeb's face lost color. "I ratted on those guys, told everything I know. I didn't have nothin' to do with the stealing, just sold the stuff."

"It's all the same. You're as guilty as they are. You're part of the ring. Don't you understand that?"

Jeb stood, hurried to the front of the cell, and grabbed a bar with each hand. His lips trembled as he nestled his face between his hands, his cheeks resting against the metal. Even though he spoke softly, Rally could hear him plead with Clay.

"I'm not as bad as them guys. You know me. Besides, we got history. You're not gonna let them put me away, are ya? I'm your cousin."

"There's nothing I can do, Jeb. You've gone too far. You're charged with assault with a firearm, although Biggs might drop that. He's got problems of his own, but you still broke the law. I can't help you. You're on your own."

Jeb stared, his mouth open. He shook his head. "No! Clay, you can't let me go to jail!"

The deputy walked away from the cell, through the office, and to the outside door. Rally and Doug watched in silence.

Deputy Adams called out. "Clay, the sheriff says he's on his way with Biggs. He said he'll be here as soon as he fills his car with gas. Shall I put Biggs next to Jeb?"

Clay turned and walked back to the desk. "Denzil, take the dirty dishes back over to Marie's. Don't let the prisoner out when you go in his cell. I need to talk to my friends here while you're gone. Take your time."

"Okay, Clay. I'll visit Marie and have a cup of coffee. Call me if you need me."

The deputy grabbed his hat from a shelf over the coat rack and hustled out the door, then rushed back in. He looked at Clay, ducked his head, retrieved the chili bowls and coffee cups, and rushed back out.

Rally sat down in a chair. Doug stood behind her. She thought they must look like two young children, waiting to hear their punishment.

"I should be furious with you two. I think you realize how your actions could have made everything go wrong. Your Keystone Cops method of apprehension leaves something to be desired. I can only be thankful that neither of you got hurt."

Doug looked at Clay, rubbed his earlobe. "Thanks, Clay. I guess there was a compliment in there somewhere."

"No, Doug, no compliment intended. Now, get out of here before I throw you in there with Jeb. Go over to Marie's and tell Deputy Adams I said he should take you over to Will's." He pointed a finger at Doug's chest. "You collect your grandmother, then have Adams take the two of you home. I'm sure Miss Eunice is beside herself with worry."

"Yes, sir." Doug walked toward the door, stopped, and looked back at the cell area.

"By the way, Clay. Where's Paul Putnam?"

"Sheriff Turner radioed me earlier that Marney brought CeCe to the jail to see him. CeCe had a bunch of calls for prescription refills, so the sheriff released him to their custody to go to the pharmacy for a few hours. He wasn't afraid of Paul running, thinks when the judge hears his story, he'll make some exceptions. People need their medicine. Marney said she would take full responsibility for him."

"Paul's not a bad person," Rally said. "His reaction was understandable, but he should have talked to CeCe instead of hiring Jeb to follow her and run Biggs out of town. He's a good man, and he's all CeCe has left. He needs a chance to make amends."

"I agree with that. Everyone deserves another chance." The deputy looked toward the jail cells. "But after so many chances—"

"Maybe Jeb will learn his lesson this time." Rally interrupted.

The deputy looked at her. "Maybe I've learned mine, too" He glanced at Doug.

"Didn't I tell you to leave?"

"I can take Doug over to Will's and pick up Eunice." Rally stood, her car keys in hand. "I have nothing better to do. After that, I'll start getting my things together for my trip back to Chicago." She looked down, fidgeted the keys between her fingers. "I can't believe I've been here such a short time. It seems much longer, and different from what I expected."

"Oh, no." Clay walked over to her. "You're not going anywhere. You stay right where you are. We are going to have a conversation."

Rally froze. "About what?"

He looked at Doug and motioned toward the door. "Go."

"Yes, sir." Doug looked at Rally, shrugged, then walked out the door.

Rally turned to look at the deputy. "If you're upset with me about today, I'm sorry. Doug was so intent on stopping Biggs, I—"

"You're in big trouble, young lady. What were you

thinking?" He stared at her, his legs straight, feet rooted to the floor.

She spread both hands out to her sides. The keys dangled from a Texas Star key ring, hooked around a finger. "Doug talked me into doing something stupid, and I almost hurt someone again. It's as much my fault as his."

"What do you mean?"

She turned away. "I tried to scare Biggs into stopping. I didn't want him to hit Blue. She means too much to me."

His face tightened. "Then why did you have her ... it, in the intersection to start with? You and Doug both have better sense than that. The two of you together can't seem to stay out of trouble. I think the best thing for you both is to stay apart until you go back to Chicago."

A moment of silence lingered between them.

"You're going to let me go back, like that? That easy?" She diverted her eyes.

"What?" He looked at her. A shadow passed across his face.

"I mean ... you said I'm in trouble. Are you not going to arrest me?"

Clay flung his hat down on the desk. "No, Rally, I will not arrest you. Ticket you, maybe, and let the judge figure it out, but I will detain you. I need to know why you avoid me. I've seen the way you look at me, but why are you keeping the door closed between us? If you're not interested, fine, but I need to know. If there's someone back in Chicago, I'll understand."

She looked down at the keys in her hand. "No, there's no one. I don't trust ... it's something, not someone." She walked to the desk, then turned to look at him. "You're a fine man, a minister. I could never live up to what you want or need. I have too much baggage, too many things—"

"Are you talking about the incident in Kansas City?"

She stood back, mouth open. "You know about that?"

"Yes. We have a mutual friend in the K.C. police

department. When you ran me off the road on your first day here, I knew you were coming. Frankly, after that, I thought it was going to be a gigantic energy drain, trying to watch after you."

"Scott Ketcham called you to watch after me?" She shook her head, slammed her fist down on the desk, frustration radiating from her in waves.

"I'm sorry, Rally, I didn't mean to invade your privacy, but I care about you, and when you kept saying things about not being good enough, about me not knowing what you'd done, I asked Scott for more details. He sent newspaper stories, some news videos. I wanted to know so I could help you."

Rally glared at him. "You have no right. You need to stay out of my life. I've worked hard to live with that, to put it behind me." She grabbed her purse and headed toward the door.

As she tried to move around him, Clay grabbed her and gathered her into his arms. She trembled. His embrace felt strong, comforting. She burrowed her face into his shoulder and wept. She could feel him press his lips to the top of her head.

"Tell me."

A soft shudder from somewhere deep inside felt liberating. "His name is Fenner. He lured me from home and family with promises of photography school and glamorous jobs. He thought I owed him because he helped me find an apartment and a job as a part-time secretary for the city. I rode to and from work with him every day. He was very nice, but every time I asked about the photography school, he made excuses, said his friend couldn't get me a scholarship until the next semester, things like that. I kept saving money, waiting.

She wiped at her tears with the back of her hand.

"He wanted to meet me for dinner one evening. Said we would talk about the school, but he followed me home ..."

"He forced his way in?" He pulled a handkerchief from his hip pocket and placed it in her hand.

"With a knife. Said if I would do what he wanted ..." She wiped her wet face.

"I kicked him in the stomach while he was trying to tie my wrists together. The knife went flying. When he let go to look for the knife, I reached behind me, got into the drawer in my nightstand, and grabbed the Beretta my brother gave me for protection. He came after me again."

"And you shot him."

She nodded. "The apartment manager heard the shots. She called 911 and then testified in court."

She dug her fingers into his arms, sobs wracked her body. Clay held her.

"But I didn't stop. I shot him three times. When the police got there, he was lying on the floor in a pool of blood." She sobbed. "I don't know why I shot him so many times. It was like I had no control. I couldn't quit."

"You did what you had to do to protect yourself from that monster. He could have come after you again. An injured animal is capable of anything. He was not the victim, you were. The court proved that."

"He lied." She gulped for air between sobs. "He lied about me, about having a relationship with me. It was such an embarrassment for me and my family. I was stupid to believe someone like him. It was shameful that I wanted to go to the school more than I wanted to honor my parents, to be with my family. I'll never get over the guilt."

He hugged her. "I'm sure your parents forgave you. I imagine they felt hurt, but they loved you unconditionally, just like God does. We all fall short, but He's never far away. All we need to do is reach out."

She pushed back from his chest, grabbed a tissue from her purse, and wiped her nose.

"When you said Sunday that God doesn't leave us, that we leave Him, that made me think about things. I'm glad I went back to Texas and spent time before my dad died. I miss him terribly and think of him every time I get into Blue. He restored her for me. He had such high hopes, wanted me to go to college and be somebody."

"You are somebody, Rally. Look what you did for CeCe and Paul Putnam. And I'm sure Doug has benefited from knowing you. I know that I have."

"Oh, Clay. Thank you. That means a lot." She put her arms around his neck and hugged him. "One thing I'm thankful for, I don't have to live with killing that man. He lived, but he's probably wandering around somewhere looking for me right now. Turns out, I wasn't the only woman he befriended. Others came forward when it appeared in the news. At least, I got him stopped, but he swore in the courtroom that he would get even."

Clay leaned in and wiped her tears with his fingers. "You don't need to worry about that anymore. They picked Fenner up early this morning in a stolen car about five miles from his cousin's house in Springfield. Scott was trying to call you during your and Doug's fiasco with Biggs."

He tipped her chin upward with a crooked finger. "He didn't get far from the State Penitentiary in a week. Seems he wasn't after you at all. He had a plane ticket to Seattle and a wad of cash on him, provided by the cousin. I figure he thought he could buy his way up to Canada or Alaska."

"I guess the cousin is in big trouble, too."

"Yeah, I suppose. He might have been doing what he thought he should. Sometimes it happens that way." He glanced over his shoulder at Jeb.

"I'm sorry Clay, for everything," she said. "I've been condescending to you, while you've been nothing but kind and patient. Monarch Moon is lucky to have you as a deputy sheriff and pastor."

He looked at her, part lawman, part minister. She saw something unsettling in his eyes.

"What's wrong, Clay? What's bothering you?"

"I have some decisions to make. With all that's happened today, this entire week, my life is going to change. I need some time to think and pray." He turned, looked at his cousin lying on the cot in his cell.

"Jeb, I'm going out for a while. Adams should be back from Doug's any minute. Anything you need?"

"I'll take a piece of cherry pie."

"This isn't the Hilton. We don't do room service. I'll bring back some deodorant, stuff like that."

"Thanks, cuz."

Clay looked at Rally, touched her hair and kissed her cheek. "Can you find your way back to Will's? Don't pack up and take off on me. I still have a ticket to write. I'm trying to decide which, out of a plethora of things, to charge you with. This has turned into a real mess." He looked around the jail.

"I don't want to lock good people up. Some of you are on the honor system tonight. I'll see if I can get Judge Smith out of his fishing hole and let him sort it out tomorrow."

"I think I can find my way. If I'm fined more than what's in my checking and savings accounts, I may have to stay and get a job to pay it off." She fluttered her eyelashes and walked toward the door.

Chapter 30

Thoughts of Clay ran through Rally's mind as she walked through the door and into Will's living room. She let her guard down while she was with him, but on the way home, she remembered who he was, and who she was not. Her heart longed to be happy with him, but that was not apt to happen.

She hung her jacket on the coat rack by the door, stopped and listened to chatter coming from the dining room. She eased her way through the doorway and looked around.

Marney and Miss Eunice sat close together at the big oak dining table, engrossed in something in front of them. Doug and Will stood, looking over the ladies' shoulders.

"Look at this one. Why, it looks like it could come up off that paper and fly away." Miss Eunice sorted through a pile of photographs.

"Hey, look at that family of ducks. You can see every feather." Will picked up the picture and held it to the light.

"What do you have there?" Rally asked as she walked to

the table.

Marney looked up and smiled. "We've had dinner, but I kept a plate warm for you. Would you like it now?"

"No, not yet. I'll rest a bit before I eat. What's got everyone so absorbed?"

Marney turned in her chair and looked up. "It's your photographs. When I took Paul and CeCe to the pharmacy, she asked me to give them to you. There must be a hundred photos here."

Eunice shuffled through the pictures until she found what she wanted.

"These are beautiful, dear. I don't think I've seen snapshots so realistic. You certainly have a knack." She held up the one in her hand. "You should enlarge and frame this one. It's beautiful enough to be on the front of a coffee-table book."

Rally looked at the picture, the beautiful Monarch butterfly she had captured in her viewfinder on the second day of her visit. That seemed a long time ago.

"She's a beauty. I wonder where she is now."

Will looked over her shoulder. "I would guess they're in Texas by now. They sure are a pretty sight."

Marney spread pictures out across the table. "Look at these, Rally. The river, the bridge, wildflowers, birds, the tree-covered mountains reflecting in the lake. You've captured the Ozarks. This is your niche, girl. You need to be a nature photographer. This is so much better than taking pictures of models, cars, and buildings."

The pictures *were* breathtaking. She had captured her subjects well and thought about how relaxed she was when she photographed what was around her that day. She loved it, and it had not seemed like work.

"Maybe you need to move here," Doug said. "Buy that cabin in the woods and open a studio. You could sell these to magazines, greeting card companies, all kinds of places. Where could you find anything more beautiful than this?"

She sighed. "It's something to think about. I *love* this area, even though I feel like I've been on a rollercoaster this week. I don't know if I could stand this much excitement all the time."

Doug tipped his head, smirked. "It's quiet around here most of the time. All this craziness happened after you and the monarchs got here. I don't know that we need you clogging up the drains in our peaceful little town."

"Douglas Carl!" Eunice glared up at her grandson.

Rally swatted him on the arm. "You've caused most of my trouble here, Douglas Carl."

Doug winced. "We're going home. I sent the deputy back to town. Will is loaning me his truck for tonight. I'll check on my truck tomorrow, see if they think they can salvage it. If not, I'll have to find something cheap, so I can go looking for a job next week. I sure can't afford a truck payment right now."

"Maybe the hospital will rehire you after all that's happened. I'm sure Clay will tell them that Biggs lied about you." Rally watched Doug carry Eunice's overnight bag and the navy dress covered by the cleaner's bag to the door.

"That would be nice. I'd love to have my job back so I can apply for the nursing program. I hope I can work part time and go to school."

Will helped Eunice with her jacket and stuck his elbow out for her to take his arm. She ignored his gesture, reached up and patted her grandson.

"You don't need to worry about tuition. I've got a little stashed away for your education."

"What?" Doug stood, mouth open. "No, Grandma. I can't let you do that."

"Well, I'm going to. You've earned it by helping an old lady with the family business." She stood on tiptoe and kissed her grandson's cheek.

Doug hugged his grandmother, then turned to Rally. "If you decide you're interested in the cabin, let me know. I'll see what I can find out for you."

"Thanks, Doug. I'll give it some thought," she said.

~ ~ ~ ~

The truck lights reflected in the picture window as Doug backed around and headed down the road. Rally watched until they were out of sight.

"I asked them to come for Sunday dinner. A kind of farewell dinner for you, I guess." Marney stood beside her friend.

"Thank you, Marney. I appreciate it. I'm going to miss everyone." She paused. "I'll have to leave right after we clean up."

"I'll ask Clay to come, and CeCe. If the judge releases Paul into my custody, I might as well include him. I can't think of a better way to keep my eye on him." Marney winked. "Not that he needs watching."

"That wouldn't be too hard to do if you ask me. He's nice looking."

"You noticed that too, huh?"

"It would be hard to miss," Rally grinned. "One other thing."

"What's that?"

"Why don't you ask Clay if there's any chance of springing Jeb for church and dinner? He's a mess, but I can't help but feel sorry for him. I'd like it if he could be with us."

"That's so sweet of you," she patted Rally on the shoulder. "I guess I can handle him one more time. He sure won't get home-cooked meals where he's going."

"Well," Rally looked back out the window at a hunter's moon. "I think Clay might like to have him here, if he can swing it with the sheriff and the judge."

"Oh, I think that could happen. That's the nice thing about a small town. Things can be a little unorthodox."

Chapter 31

Deputy Clay Woods wrangled a herd of people through the door and into the courtroom of Judge Raymond Smith. Clay's best efforts at control were useless. The noisy group made more commotion than a barn dance on Saturday night. Judge Smith, in a plaid flannel shirt and Carhartt overalls, stared down at him from the bench and twisted the end of a thick white mustache.

"What's going on here, Clay? Couldn't you lock up this menagerie until I get back from fishing on Monday? I just got my first bite when you called. Had to come in and take my waders off." He rubbed a hand across his flushed, round face.

Clay looked at the steely-eyed octogenarian. Raymond Smith had occupied the bench for as long as he could remember. The voters put him back in the courthouse, even when someone opposed him. He insisted at the first of each year he would retire before the first of the next, but nothing much happened in their sleepy little community. When it did, it most often was an open-and-shut case. Clay supposed the man was as close to being retired as anyone could be and still draw a paycheck.

Sheriff Taylor said he expected Ray would be there until he became senile or died. Whichever came first.

"Well, Judge, we've got kind of a mess here. I don't quite know where to start. It's been an unusual week." He looked around at his charges.

"Looks like it. Please explain, Deputy."

"I would like to start with the worst offense."

The judge sat back, crossed his arms over his ample chest, nodded his head. "That's as good a place as any."

A low rumble started, then rose into a loud uproar as the crowd argued about which offense was worse.

Jeb jumped from his seat and pointed at Biggs. "Mine wasn't the worst offense. He flat out tried to kill that boy." He pointed at Doug. "Tell him, Doug."

Biggs stood, pointed a finger, and shook it at Jeb. "That's a lie. I did not try to kill anyone." He turned and looked at the judge. "That idiot tried to shoot me."

Jeb planted a fist on each hip and glared back. "You can't prove that I tried to shoot you. I was hunting outside that secluded cabin, slipped in mud, and fell flat down. The gun went off on its own. Nobody ever stays in them outer cabins at the motel, anyways. I didn't think it was a big deal."

He relaxed his fists, lowered his arms, and pointed at Biggs. "You must have something to hide." He turned toward the bench. "It was an accident, Ray, ah, Judge."

Biggs slammed a hand down on the chair. "I did nothing for which to be arrested. All I know is I was being chased by that woman over there," he pointed at Rally, "and that insane man there," he pointed at Doug. "Everyone knows he's reckless. That's why he got fired from the ambulance service."

Doug stared across at Biggs, bristled. "I got fired

because you lied and set me up. You wanted me out, gone, one way or another."

Judge Smith pounded his gavel. "Stop! Clay! Get these people under control, then you tell me what's going on here."

Clay nodded. "Yes, sir." He turned around and scowled at the three men. "That's enough." The low rumble ceased. "Sit down. All three of you. Everyone, please be quiet while I try to make sense of this for the judge."

"That would be nice, Deputy." The older man shifted in his chair.

"Your Honor—"

"Oh, cut the formality, Clay, and get on with it. I don't have all weekend, as you well know."

"Yes, sir, well, someone hit Doug on the head, pushed his truck into the lake. Tire tracks in the mud near where his truck sat match tire tracks on Biggs's SUV."

"Is that a new vehicle?"

"Yes, sir," Biggs answered.

"Are those the same tires that came on the vehicle?"

"Yes, your Honor."

"All right, Clay. How many other automobiles might have the same tread as that?"

"We're not sure, Sir. I don't have any reports back from the State yet. What I have are photos and casts of tire tracks from the scene, and they look the same."

"So, we don't know for absolute certain it was Mr. Biggs here that did it."

"Well, nothing for sure yet, but I think I'll have evidence of that soon."

"If I may, your Honor," Biggs nodded toward Rally and Doug.

"They drove across the road in front of me. She turned her car sideways and blocked my path."

Clay saw Rally's jaw tighten. This was not good, but before he could put a hand on her shoulder, she stepped up to Biggs, stood a hair's width from his face, nose to nose.

"Your Honor, I was trying to slow this slick, manipulating, gold digging liar down, so Deputy Woods could catch up and apprehend him." She looked back over her shoulder at the judge. "And just so you know, the man threatened me."

Biggs crossed his arms and sneered. "Threatened you? When, my dear girl, did I ever threaten you?"

"At the convenience store on South Maple. You know you did, in so many words. Told me to keep my nose out of things or else."

The judge leaned forward. "Or else what? Did he threaten to harm you?"

Rally's eyes sent daggers at Biggs. "He implied it, your Honor."

Judge Smith pounded his gavel again. "We digress. This sounds like junior high school stuff to me." He turned to Clay. "Is that the best you got? I thought you were going to start with the worst offense."

Clay lowered his head, then looked up. "Jeb Andrews has admitted to an offense. He got involved with the ring of thieves that's been plaguing the county. He was helping them—"

Jeb jumped up from his seat. "But I cooperated with the law." He turned to his cousin. "Tell him, Clay. I told you about every one of them guys. They didn't tell me they stole the stuff. I just let them use my outbuildings to store it. They paid me rent." He shrugged, looked at Clay. "Well, ah, I wasn't sure what they were doin'."

The judge rubbed a hand across his forehead. "The Prosecuting Attorney is on vacation. I'm sorry, Clay, but I think you need to keep Jeb in your jail until the P.A. gets back. Jeb seems harmless, but he could be a flight risk. When I get back on Monday, we'll see about bail. What's next?"

"Jeb may or may not have shot into Biggs' cabin to

scare him out of town, but I have footprints from the cabin that match Jeb's shoes. I also found a spent shotgun shell that matches one I found in Jeb's possession. Paul Putnam paid him to scare Biggs."

"What? Paul Putnam?" The judge directed his attention to the pharmacist. "Paul. What on earth? You're one of the most upstanding citizens in Monarch Moon."

"I meant no harm. Jeb was only supposed to scare Biggs away from CeCe."

Marney stood up. "Your Honor, may I approach the bench?"

"You're Will Darnell's niece." The adjudicator tipped his head to the side and frowned.

"Yes, sir." She swallowed. "I'm Marney Phillips."

"Don't tell me you're mixed up in all this mess."

"Yes, sir, I am. Miss Chandler is my best friend. I know Paul Putnam from the pharmacy and through CeCe." She pointed at the young woman who clung to her father's hand. "I know everyone else here but Mr. Biggs, and I know who he is."

"So?" Judge Smith waited.

"I would like to be counsel for all but Jeb Andrews and Mr. Biggs, at least until they can get a proper attorney."

The judge rolled his eyes, threw his hands up, and fell back into his chair. "Mother of Pearl."

Clay moved toward the bench and watched for signs of life. At last, the man sat up and looked at Marney.

"Please tell me, Ms. Phillips. What makes you think you are qualified to speak on their behalf?"

Will stood. "I've had about enough of this nonsense, Ray. I'll tell you how she's qualified, then we can get these mavericks in jail and get you back to your fishin'. Maybe I'll join you." He shuffled up to the bench.

"Marney here was nearly through law school and had to quit because she ran out of money. She's been stayin' with me ever since. She's gonna' go back and finish as soon as she gets the money together, right, Marney?"

"Ah, well, I guess you could say that." She looked at Will, then the judge.

Will chuckled. "Heck, Ray, she may get your job someday."

Eunice, enlivened by Will's actions, headed toward Biggs, stared up at him and scowled. "Shame on you, young man, trying to steal property from old folks and taking advantage of young women." She shook her finger in his face. "And trying to kill my grandson because he wouldn't let you talk me into selling out to you?"

"I didn't try to kill your grandson, madam," Biggs snarled at her. "I only wanted to frighten him ..." His face turned red. He looked first at the judge, then Clay, then made a quick pivot to face Doug.

"What I did is nothing compared to him kidnapping Miss Chandler—in her own car, I might add—and making her stay in a secluded cabin all night." He turned to the judge. "Now that, your Honor, is questionable intention if I ever heard it."

Doug rushed to Biggs and grabbed him by the shirt collar. "Because I was hiding from you, you sorry excuse for a man. How did you know about that, anyway?"

"That's enough, Doug." Clay pulled him away from Biggs.

"Word gets around." Biggs smirked.

The judge leaned forward and looked at Marney. "Out of curiosity, Miss Phillips, what is your recommendation?"

"I recommend, sir, that Doug's grandmother, Eunice Hargrove, have custody of him until further notice, Rally Chandler to Deputy Woods's custody, and I will be responsible for Paul Putnam. Mr. Biggs should seek counsel as soon as possible." She looked at Jeb. "Same for him."

"Well." Judge Smith settled back into his black leather chair. "I thank you for your opinion, young lady, but I think this is all a bunch of hogwash."

A collective gasp issued from the Gallery.

"I think the only legitimate problem here is Jeb. I'm sorry, Clay, but you need to lock him up. We'll hash out his charges when the prosecuting attorney gets back." He stared at the rest of the group.

"It seems to me there is no proof that Mr. Biggs, as loathsome as he may be to you all, tried to kill anyone." He turned his attention to Biggs. "You may go, but stay in town until Officer Woods gets the results from the crime lab."

He turned his attention to Rally. "I think the air somehow changed when you came to Monarch Moon, young lady. These strange happenings seem to have started after your arrival. I hear your vacation is nearly over. That's probably a good thing."

She moved toward the bench. "But your Honor. Please remember there was a full moon when I came, and the Monarch butterfly migration was happening. You know what that means. It wasn't anything I did."

"You're kidding me." He issued a heavy sigh. "You bought into that legend, or is it a handy excuse for you right now?"

A low murmur started in the gallery. Will and Eunice stepped forward.

"Can you prove it isn't so, Ray?" Will asked.

"Yes, Raymond," Eunice chimed in. "I've known you all my life. You can't deny every time it happens, there's some strange goings on."

She turned to Rally. "This dear sweet girl did nothing to cause any of this. She takes the most beautiful pictures." She dug in her bag. "Here." She handed some photographs up to the judge. "Look at these."

He shuffled through the images of wildlife, flowers, and fauna. "Nice, very nice." Then he directed his attention back to the group in front of him.

"Clay, do you have objection to any of this?"

"No sir, I guess that let everyone off the hook but Jeb and Paul. I'll make sure Jeb's detained until the P.A. gets back. Everyone else can go."

The judge turned to Rally. "I understand Miss Chandler is leaving Sunday."

She looked at Clay, then at the judge. "Yes, I'm leaving on Sunday, but I plan to come back. Maybe when I do, you would allow me to photograph your fishing spot."

"Hmm." The judge rubbed his chin. "Maybe, if you promise not to tell anyone where it is."

"Never." She crossed her heart.

He eyed Biggs. "You hang around town until those reports come back from the state, you hear? Let the Deputy know where you're staying." He pointed at him. "Now, get out of my courtroom."

"My pleasure, Your Honor." Biggs hurried to the door and left.

Clay looked at Doug, who lifted his shoulders and shrugged.

"And Miss Phillips," he absently tapped the arm of his chair.

Marney sat straight up. "Yes, sir?"

"I appreciate you volunteering to watch over Mr. Putnam, but I think the two of you can watch over each other without my help." He turned his attention to the rest of the group.

Judge Raymond Smith pounded his gavel. "Cases dismissed for now. Go home, everybody."

Chapter 32

S unday was a gorgeous fall day, with a clear blue sky and bright sunshine, a day like Rally and Marney remembered from their childhood together in Texas. The whole town turned out for the morning service.

Everyone took his or her usual place in the pews. Rally sat on Marney's right, with Paul Putnam on her left. Rally noticed their arms were touching. Will waited outside for Doug and Miss Eunice. CeCe stood at the back of the church with the rest of the choir. Pastor Woods stood with them, Bible in hand.

The steeple bell rang three times. Myrna Dodson began the processional "Come Thou Fount of Every Blessing." The choir and minister started single file up the center aisle.

Doug, Eunice, and Will hurried through the door, jostled around Clay and the choir, and rushed down the aisle toward seats on the right side.

Myrna Dodson sat at the organ, decked out in a bright orange dress, with a matching yellow and orange hat. Two feathers waved at the congregation as she bobbed her head in time with the music and sang with an overpowering high soprano voice. Her lipstick screamed jack-o'-lantern orange. She was all smiles until she looked out at the congregation and stared, dumbfounded, as Will sat down beside Eunice and stretched an arm across the back of the pew behind her. The music came to an abrupt halt.

Pastor Woods stopped short and looked up at the organist. The choir bumped into each other like a row of standing dominos flicked by a single finger. Myrna composed herself and proceeded with the hymn, but she was not singing.

After the service, members of the community walked up to Rally, said their goodbyes, and asked her to come back and visit. Rally tensed as Clay walked toward her, but he turned instead to Marney and Will.

"I have a meeting with the church board," he said. "I'll be along as soon as we're finished. Don't wait on me for dinner. I'll catch up when I get there."

"Are you kiddin? You know how long it takes her to fry up enough chicken for all of us? I'm sure you got plenty of time."

Marney swatted at Will with a church bulletin clutched in her hand. "That's because you keep stealing legs off the platter and I have to keep frying more." She turned to Eunice and Doug. "Come on, you two. We'll head for the house and get this goodbye party started."

Rally walked with Doug to Jeb's old beat-up truck parked next to Blue. She watched Will cup Eunice's elbow in the palm of his hand and guide her across the parking lot.

"It's nice of Jeb to loan you his truck until you get yours running."

Doug nodded. "Yeah. I didn't think there was much chance of borrowing a little blue Mustang convertible to drive."

"Fat chance I'd loan my car to a kidnapper." She crossed

to the convertible to catch up with Marney, Paul, and CeCe.

Will guffawed as he helped Eunice into the truck. "Guess she shut you up, bad boy." He jigged awkwardly around Doug, singing: "Bad boy, bad boy."

Rally watched Clay disappear into the church. "What do you suppose that's all about?"

Marney shrugged. "I don't know, but there isn't a scheduled meeting for today. Something must have come up. Perhaps Clay will tell us about it when he gets to the house."

"I can't believe it's been a week," Marney said. "It seems you just got here."

"Well, it's been a busy week and not at all what I expected." Rally's attempt to laugh was half-hearted. "I have to go back to Chicago to rest up."

"Yeah, go back and tell your friends about your exciting escapades in the Ozarks." Marney looked at Rally. "I hope you miss us a little."

"I'll miss you a lot. All of you." She opened the door and slid under the steering wheel.

"All of us? Especially Clay, maybe?" Marney got into the car and fastened her seatbelt.

"Yes, I'll miss him too. He's a good man." Rally sighed as she drove out of the parking lot.

The ride home was quiet. Paul and CeCe's conversation in the backseat was too low to be heard in the front.

~ ~ ~ ~

After they got back to the house and settled, Will helped Rally load her bags into the Mustang. "This is a right nice little car you got here." He pulled his shirtsleeve over his hand and polished a spot on the hood.

"Yeah, my daddy worked hard and spent a lot of time restoring it. I was too young and stupid to understand he did it with love. All I could think about was getting in it and driving away from him. I wish he could know how much I understand that now."

"Oh, I'm sure he does." He patted her shoulder. "He knew it then."

The sound of a car engine distracted them. They turned to watch a Hayes County Sheriff's car park in front of the house. Will walked toward the vehicle. "Morning, Sheriff. You're right on time for Sunday dinner."

Sheriff Turner struggled to squeeze out of the front seat, then opened the back door for a handcuffed Jeb.

"Marney called and asked if he could come for dinner. She invited me too. My wife's whole family is at our house again today." He chewed on a wad of gum as he guided Jeb through the gate and toward the front door.

"You must have seen them. Her brother snored through the whole service. Downright embarrassing, it was. I'm glad I was sittin' at the back with Jeb. Only way I can get any peace is to work." He limped into the house, his hand on the detainee's shoulder.

"I suppose you'll behave yourself in here, won't you, Jeb?" He slipped the cuffs onto his gun belt and removed his hat.

"Yep." Jeb rubbed his wrists. "I don't plan on causing Clay any more shame. I'll take my punishment like a man." He looked over his shoulder at Will, then down at the floor.

The sheriff hung his Western hat on a peg behind the door, then settled into a comfortable chair and pointed at the sofa next to him. "Sit over here where I can see you. I don't want to take any chances on you changing your mind and making a break for it."

"Don't worry, Sheriff," Will said. "If you fall asleep after dinner, I'll be happy to swat him if he gets out of line." He looked at Jeb and winked.

Jeb grinned. "Yeah, you and whose army, old man?"

Rally carried a tray of iced tea in and sat it on the table. "In case anyone would like a glass before dinner."

The sheriff reached over, took a glass, and added sugar. "I'm sure gonna miss Clay as our minister, but he's going to make a good sheriff when he finishes up some courses at the State Patrol Academy. Can't believe I talked him into letting me retire and him take my job. He's a slam dunk to win the election."

Rally turned around and walked back into the room and stared at Sheriff Turner. "What did you say?"

"Oops, didn't you all know? Clay's going to take classes at the State Patrol Academy. He completed the arrangements Friday."

"No, I didn't." She looked back and forth between Will and Jeb. "Did you all know this?"

Jeb shrugged. "He never tells me nothin'. I might as well be a speck on the wall."

"I knew he was thinkin' about it." Will scratched his chin. "Doesn't come as any shock to me, though. He's had that itch for a while. The only thing that kept him from doin' it was the church. I suppose he finally justified it in his mind."

Will took a glass of tea. "Is this Marney's sweet tea? If it is, Sheriff, you might should have asked before you added sugar."

"The sweeter the better, I say." Sheriff Turner looked out the window. "Here comes Clay now … and who's that?"

Rally hurried into the kitchen, but turned and craned her neck around the doorway as Clay walked inside wearing a pair of Wranglers and a plaid Western shirt. Without the uniform, or the slacks, dress shirt, and tie he wore for church, he looked like a regular guy, a cowboy. She liked the look.

He moved aside, held the door open as a pretty woman walked in. She was tall, with red hair and emerald-green eyes that took in the room. Her skin, the color of pearls, was flawless. A softness about her face looked like a smile that never faded. She was backlit in the doorway, making the white mohair sweater she wore stand out. It gave her the gentleness of an angel. She wore knee-high brown leather boots and jeans.

Rally took a deep breath. Her first thought was Clay's old girlfriend, who left with no explanation. Could she have returned? He seemed happy to be in her company. She slid behind the doorjamb and watched. Marney walked up behind her.

"Who is that? Is she Clay's ex-fiancée?"

Marney leaned in and propped her chin on Rally's shoulder. "Never saw her before. This must be a new one." She straightened, swatted at Rally with the tea towel she was carrying, threw it over her shoulder, and walked straight into the living room.

"Hello, I'm Marney. Welcome."

Clay guided the woman into the room. "Everybody, I want you to meet your new pastor. This is Shannon O'Day." A collective murmur rippled through the house.

"Shannon arrived too late to be introduced to the congregation this morning, but she signed a contract a few minutes ago at the board meeting. This may be a surprise to some of you, but I put my resignation in several weeks ago. The board wanted to keep it quiet because they thought I would change my mind. I'm sorry if it's a shock." He turned to the new pastor. "I thought it would be nice to bring Shannon along for dinner. I knew she'd be welcome."

"Of course she is." Marney turned to her uncle. "We'll be eating in a few minutes. Uncle Will, introduce our guest to everyone, please, and give her one of those glasses of sweet tea on the table." She looked at the new arrival. "Please excuse me while I finish up."

The new minister beamed. "May I help?"

"It's all done. We've got it under control." A broad smile spread across her face as she turned and headed back to the kitchen. When she walked by Rally, she swatted her again with the tea towel. "Hey, girl. Help me carry this food to the dining room." She grinned at her friend. "You snooze, you lose."

Rally stared at her. "You knew."

"Of course. I know everything, but I don't tell." She gave Rally a gentle push toward the food waiting to be served.

Within minutes, steaming bowls of sides with platters of fried chicken and meatloaf were on the table. Everyone sat down, then held hands while Clay prayed.

"Lord, we ask you to bless this food, and thank you for your continued blessings in our lives. Thank you for all these good friends and families who are together here ...."

Rally waited. She felt anxious. Why was Clay hesitating?

"We ask, Lord, for your guidance as we start down fresh paths, each of us in our own way. Help us see the opportunities before us, and that we do your will in all things. And we pray for your protection over Miss Rally as she travels back to Chicago, and if it be Your will, that she return to us soon."

Rally felt her heart quiver when he spoke her name. He wanted her to return. She wished she could slide her shaking hands under the table.

"We thank you for our new pastor, Reverend O'Day, and ask that you bless her ministry here in Monarch Moon. In Jesus' name, we pray."

"Amen!" Will shouted. "Now, pass that chicken over here." He tucked a napkin in the neck of his shirt and sat with a knife clutched in one hand and a fork in the other.

Miss Eunice jabbed him in the ribs with her elbow. "Well, ain't you the worst mannered thing I've ever seen? Quit acting like an old hick." Laughter changed the mood from serious to jovial.

Jeb slapped his leg. "Guess she told you, Will." He stirred more sugar into his iced tea, took a homemade yeast roll and passed the basket to Sheriff Turner.

"You watch it there, fella," Will said. "I might have to put a few knots on your head before the sheriff here hauls you back off to the jail."

"*You* watch it, Will." Sheriff Turner pointed the tines of his fork at the older man. "I can't have you messing with my prisoner."

"Uncle Will, please." Marney looked at Paul and CeCe sitting near the end of the table.

"Well, it ain't like nobody here don't know who all's going to jail. It's not a secret. I's having a little fun, that's all." He helped himself to the mashed potatoes.

"Will!" She glared at her uncle.

"It's okay, Marney." Paul looked around the table. "I appreciate your concern, but I'm as guilty as Jeb. I might as well have fired that gun myself. You all don't know how ashamed I am of being so stupid. I hope all of you, as well as this entire community, will forgive me." He looked at his daughter. "Especially you, CeCe."

"It's okay, Daddy." CeCe placed her hand on her father's and squeezed it.

Clay turned to the pharmacist. "You've had a lot of sadness, Paul. What you did was not right, but I think it was a knee-jerk reaction to circumstances you didn't know how to handle." He looked at his cousin.

"But Jeb's problem isn't solely associated with you. He was involved in a more serious crime. He'll have to take responsibility for once in his life and suffer the consequences of his poor judgment." His look was stern, his jaw set.

Rally watched Clay's focus return to his plate of food, saw lines in his face she had not noticed before. He looked tired. Was she the only one who saw the sadness in him?

"That's right, Deputy." Sheriff Turner buttered an ear of corn, then pointed the knife at Jeb. "But, as ornery as you've been your whole life, I've always kind of liked you.

I hope they teach you something in jail that you can make a decent living with when you get out. I suppose there's enough folk around here that would give you a chance if you cleaned up good and asked them for a job."

"Thanks, Sheriff." Jeb leaned his head on the officer's shoulder. "I kinda like you, too."

Will slapped his knee and laughed. "Watch out there, Sheriff. He'll be wanting to come live with you when he gets out."

Sheriff Turner pushed Jeb away. "Stop that." He brushed his shoulder with his napkin. "But if he could put up with my wife's family, he's a better man than I am."

Rally looked for expressions that might betray what Clay was thinking. He sat tall and straight. He looked up, caught her watching him, held her gaze for a moment, then put his napkin down and looked around the table.

She held her breath and waited.

"You all know now that I'm making some changes in my life, I think for the better all around. I love both the ministry and law enforcement, but I can't continue to do both.

"Monarch Moon deserves more than a part-time minister. The need is for someone full time. I gave the board a list of my recommendations. They chose Reverend O'Day." He nodded at the new pastor.

"I also feel that if I can't guide *my* family," he took a sip of water, "how can I guide an entire congregation?"

"Ah, cuz, this is all my fault." Jeb dropped his head and rubbed the back of his neck.

"No. It's not all your fault. It's partly mine. I let you get by with too much for too long. I didn't make you take responsibility when you were young. We all felt sorry for you because your parents were gone. I let you down. You might not be in this position if I had done what I should have."

Rally stared at Clay. What an amazing man. So kind and

forgiving. And he had shown her every bit of that. She was insensitive, tried to push him away, and now she understood. He was everything she needed and had ever wanted in a man. She hoped it wasn't too late.

The rest of the meal was a mixture of small talk, getting acquainted with the new pastor, congratulations to Clay on his decision to run for sheriff, and regrets about Rally leaving. Eunice passed out pieces of her sweet potato pie and Marney's burnt sugar cake. Finally, the men complimented the women on the fine meal, and adjourned to the screened-in back porch for coffee.

Reverend O'Day offered to help. Marney handed her a tea towel, and a stream of chatter ensued. After Rally put away the last of the pans, she stood and flexed her shoulders. "Well, I guess I'd better get on my way. I can be in St. Louis shortly after dark. I have a cousin I'm going to spend the night with, then go on home, ah, Chicago, tomorrow." She corrected herself because this felt more like home than Chicago ever would.

Eunice wrapped some leftover chicken and placed it into a small Styrofoam cooler.

"Here, dear. I'm also going to send some of my pie with you." She cut a large wedge and slid it into a plastic container. "Otherwise, that old geezer will eat it all. He doesn't need it. He's getting fat from all the baking I've done here."

Rally and Marney looked at each other and smiled. Rally accepted the cooler and gave Eunice a hug. "Thank you. You're such a sweetheart. I'm going to miss your home cooking."

Eunice wiped a tear from her cheek. "Well, look at me. I'm getting all blubbery. I wasn't going to do this, but, oh, well." She pulled Rally close and hugged her. "Are you sure this is what you want to do? You could stay here with us."

"I need to go. I have nothing to fear now. The bad guy is

behind bars again and not likely to be out for a long time. I have an apartment with everything I own in it, other than what I brought with me."

"Well, isn't what you brought with you all you need?" Marney dabbed at tears with a tissue. "You could stay with us until you decide what you want to do. I know you like Monarch Moon better than Chicago." She pointed at Rally's jeans and gold turtleneck. "And you're finding about everything you need to wear in my skinny closet."

Rally looked down at the jeans and laughed. "Oops. I'll get these to you as soon as I can."

"Thanksgiving." Eunice squeezed between them. "You can come and bring them. I may have dinner at my place, or maybe Will might want us to have it here. He has more room. Either way, I'll be making my homemade noodles, cornbread stuffing, candied sweet potatoes, pecan pie—"

"Stop!" Rally threw a hand up in protest. "You're making me hungry, and I just ate." She grabbed Eunice and hugged her. "I will be back for Thanksgiving. No doubt about it. I'll have all my scheduled photo shoots completed by then and I won't accept any more. There's no place I would rather be than here. I need to tie up loose ends and clean my apartment. There are things there I need to dust off and put back into use."

"And what might that be?" Marney asked.

"My dad's Bible, and his daily devotional. That's all I have of him, except Blue. I need some guidance right now." She collected her keys from the counter.

"Doug is checking on that cabin for me. Who knows what might happen? I could have a home and studio all in one if they accept my offer."

Marney hugged her. "Oh, Rally. I hope so."

"Hey, you women still in that kitchen?" Will stuck his head through the door.

"Doug wants to get his grandma home. It's probably way past her bedtime, anyway."

Eunice took her apron off and hung it on a hook by the stove. "You ornery old toad. I don't go to bed with the chickens like you do and I don't have a bedtime. I do as I please, and I'm not fixin' to change that."

Will scratched his head. "What is that all about? You think I have it in my head to change your life, Eunice Hargrove? I like mine fine the way it is right now. I don't need no complications in it, either."

Clay walked into the kitchen. "What's going on in here? Will, are you behaving yourself with these women? You're not causing trouble, are you?"

"Nah." He rubbed his head and started toward the back door. "That widder woman gets some crazy ideas, that's all."

Eunice threw her shoulders back. "Men. There's no figuring them out." She gave Rally a last hug. "We'll see you Thanksgiving, if not before." She started toward the door to the living room when her grandson burst through and scanned the kitchen.

"Hey, Rally. I got a call a minute ago from the owner of the cabin. He accepted your offer. You can rent it with an option to buy whenever you're ready. He's glad someone wants it who will take care of it and appreciate its original beauty."

Rally could feel the excitement building in the room. She felt as if her chest would explode. Everyone waited for a reaction. All she could do was stare at Doug, her hand over her heart.

Marney touched her arm. "Rally?" She scooted a stool away from the kitchen bar and took the cooler from her hand. "Do you want to sit down?"

"Does this mean you're staying?" Clay stepped forward to stand close to her. "That you're going to be in Monarch Moon permanently?"

"She was saying her goodbyes." Marney looked at Clay. "I hope Doug's news means she's going to make Monarch

Moon her home after she's finished her business in Chicago. She never was one to leave a mess behind." She motioned to Doug and Eunice. "Let's leave the two of them alone to talk."

She shooed Doug back through the door, and Eunice followed. Rally called after them. "Thank you, Doug. I appreciate what you've done to help me make a deal on the cabin. I owe you a finder's fee or something."

Doug called back from the other room. "No problem. I'm glad you're going to be hanging out with me again. Lots of adventures for us to share in the future."

"Life is full of surprises, isn't it?" Clay stared at her, reached out and touched her hand. She did not back away. This time, she melted into his arms. He tucked a finger under her chin and tilted her head upward, then brushed her lips with his. "I've been praying for this."

~ ~ ~ ~

The late afternoon sun cast golden rays through tall oak trees as the Sunday dinner guests disbanded and headed their separate ways. Before Sheriff Taylor returned Jeb to his jail cell, he allowed him to say goodbye to everyone—especially the new pastor.

"Ah, Reverend O'Day," Jeb called from the back seat of the patrol car. "A word?"

Everyone watched him stretch his neck through the open window of the cruiser to enjoy the new pastor's walk across the lawn.

She bent to his level, pulled hair the color of burnished copper away from her face. "Yes, Jeb?"

All anyone could hear were mumbles from him and see an occasional head nod from the pastor, but when Reverend O'Day patted him on the shoulder and walked away, Jeb was all smiles as he watched her stroll back to her Jeep.

"What do you suppose that was about?" Rally watched

the patrol car leave.

Clay reached for her hand. "I expect Jeb told her he was a sinner and asked her to pray for him and probably invited her to visit him at the jail. My cousin doesn't miss a trick, especially when he thinks he can get sympathy from a pretty woman."

"Well, maybe he's sincere. I hope so. Or maybe she can help him find a better path." Rally turned her attention to the others heading for their own cars and home.

Paul and CeCe walked to their car at the edge of the driveway. Will and Eunice visited while Doug loaded her casserole dishes and pie plates, now scrubbed clean and ready to be used again. Rally and Clay watched Will plant a quick kiss on the top of Eunice's head.

Rally waved goodbye as the cars left the parking area. She turned to Clay. "I'd better hit the road and be on my way so I can make it to St. Louis at a decent time."

"Yeah. Me, too." He smiled at her. "I'm spending the night in Rolla, so I can get some details handled and be back here before my shift starts at noon. That's a three-hour drive. You might be ready for a coffee break by then?"

She felt her heartbeat quicken. "Sure, of course, I'd like that."

"So would I." Clay grinned, then went inside to get the ice chest for her.

Will shuffled over and wrapped an arm around her shoulders and gave her a gentle bear hug. "There's something you need to know about that cabin, young lady. I know a secret, but you can't tell anyone."

She nodded. "I understand. I won't tell." She looked into his rheumy eyes. "You're going to trust your secret with a girl from New York City?"

Merriment danced across his face. "After I found out you're from East Texas, I didn't mind you so much. In fact, I got right fond of you. You're not a Yankee, by any means."

Will whispered in her ear. She grabbed his shoulders, kissed him on the forehead, and hugged him. "I can't believe this, Will. Thank you so much for sharing, and I will guard your secret well."

Chapter 33

Rally and Clay sat side by side on the hood of the Mustang in a vacant parking lot in Rolla. They sipped fast food coffee. Clay sat his cup behind him and reached for Rally's hand. She smiled.

"What did Will mutter into your ear when I came out with your road food? He looked serious, and you looked ecstatic."

She shivered, scooted closer. "It's Will's story to tell. I can't. I promised him."

His arm encircled her. He took the coffee from her hand and sat it down next to his.

She put an arm around his neck and pulled his head down to hers. "I was so afraid, but now I know, even if you remained in the ministry, I could be there for you. Monarch Moon taught me that. I'm more than I thought I could be after—"

"Shh." He placed a finger across her lips. "That happened then. It didn't change you inside. This is now,

Rally. We are now."

Tears formed but did not spill. "I tried so hard not to like you, but I think I'm at your mercy."

"I'm glad you got the cabin and that you're coming back to Monarch Moon." He stroked her cheek with the tips of his fingers.

"As soon as I can get things finished in Chicago, and the cabin's ready. I think it will make a great place to live and work." She stretched upward and kissed his cheek.

They slid off the hood of the car into an embrace, then walked around the Mustang, their arms around each other. He opened the driver's side door for her.

"So you'll be back for Thanksgiving?"

"Yes. I'll see you Thanksgiving."

She watched the light in his eyes as he gently drew her into his arms and lowered his lips to hers. The moment was electric. She responded in a way she had never felt before, as though her body could fuse to his.

Who are you, woman, and what have you done with Rally Chandler?

She melted into his arms and kissed him back with such passion it shocked her.

~ ~ ~ ~

Clay Woods' Ford pickup pulled back onto I-44 ahead of her. She followed him onto the Interstate, looked up at the early evening sky and smiled.

"A lot happened this week, Lord. Thank you for taking the bad and turning it into good and thank you for all the love I found in Monarch Moon."

A single Monarch butterfly landed on the steering wheel. She pulled over to the side of the road, bent her finger and watched the insect find its way onto her knuckle.

"You've fallen behind, you beautiful little creature. Go find the rest of your kaleidoscope. There's a tree in the woods behind my cabin, but don't tell anyone. It's a secret only Will and I know."

She got out of the car and raised her finger to the gentle breeze. The butterfly moved its wings, spiraled into the sky, then turned south.

"Safe journey, little one."

A Word About the Monarchs

The Monarch butterfly population is steadily declining. Loss of habitat and overuse of pesticides are the primary reasons. In Mexico, where they winter in the mountain forests, agriculture and tourism are reducing their roosting locations. Overuse of pesticides everywhere is killing their food supply.

The monarchs require milkweed to survive. The larvae eat only that plant. Adult monarchs feed on a variety of nectar bearing flowers, but they lay their eggs exclusively on milkweed.

If you're interested in saving the Monarch butterfly population, please go to www.saveourmonarchs.org for more information. If you have space, please plant milkweed for the larvae to eat. A variety of bright-colored flowers will not only feed the adult monarchs, but all species of butterfly.

Watching the Monarch migration from my deck one Ozarks morning was an event with nature I will never forget. I hope you get to experience their travels someday, as well.

About the Author

Bonnie K. Tesh is coauthor of the inspirational book, *I'll Push, You Steer; the Definitive Guide to Stumbling Through Life with Blinders On.* Her work has appeared in anthologies, regional magazines, and newspapers. She has won awards for her short stories, memoirs, and poetry.

Raised in the Missouri Ozarks, a lot of her writing reflects that region's atmosphere.

She and her husband, Richard, spent twenty-one years living in a quiet cove on Table Rock Lake, near Branson, Missouri, where she saw her first Monarch butterfly migration. They now live in Joplin, Missouri.